$10.90

W9-DJH-031

NC

JUI

SPIRITS, SPOOKS, AND OTHER SINISTER CREATURES

SPIRITS, SPOOKS, AND OTHER SINISTER CREATURES

SELECTED BY HELEN HOKE

A GROLIER COMPANY

FRANKLIN WATTS | 1984
NEW YORK | LONDON | TORONTO | SYDNEY

Library of Congress Cataloging in Publication Data
Main entry under title:

Spirits, spooks, and other sinister creatures.

Summary: A collection of horror stories by
contemporary writers and old masters.
1. Horror tales, American.   2. Horror tales, English.
3. Children's stories, American.   4. Children's stories,
English.   [1. Horror stories.   2. Short stories]
I. Hoke, Helen, 1903–
PZ5.S7535   1984   [Fic]   83-21603
ISBN 0-531-04769-5

CONTENTS

SPIRITS, SPOOKS, AND OTHER SINISTER CREATURES

ACKNOWLEDGMENTS

The selections in this book are used by permission of and special arrangements with the proprietors of their respective copyrights, who are listed below. The editor's and publisher's thanks go to all who have made this collection possible.

The editor and publisher have made every effort to trace ownership of all material contained herein. It is their belief that the necessary permissions from publishers, authors, and authorized agents have been obtained in all cases. In the event of any questions arising as to the use of any material, the editor and publisher express regret for any error unconsciously made and will be pleased to make the necessary corrections in future editions of the book.

"The Bantam Phantom," by Lael J. Littke. © 1971 by Lael J. Littke. First published in *Ellery Queen's Mystery Magazine.* Reprinted by permission of Larry Sternig Literary Agency.

"The Dance of the Thirteen Skeletons," by Jack Prelutsky. From *Nightmares* by Jack Prelutsky. Copyright © 1976 by Jack Pre-

ABOUT THIS BOOK

Here are some strange and inexplicable phenomena! You will meet disembodied spirits on their nightly sprees, as well as some otherworldly presences on mysterious and weird missions. You will witness some malevolent and even a few benign visitors from the dark past. You will also encounter sinister creatures along their terrifying trails—creatures who bring nothing but danger to those who cross their paths.

The tales in this collection will take you to old castles and stately mansions and the house next door; to the sands of Egypt and the meadows of midwestern United States; to dusty little shops and sophisticated city restaurants. Some of the writers represented here are old masters in the art of terror; the rest are talented new writers.

In Saki's blood-freezing tale, "The Wolves of Cernogratz," scores of wolves from far and wide come before a castle, howling in chorus. The truth behind this terrifying phenomenon is known *only* to the old governess in the castle.

In Robert Bloch's tale, "A Most Unusual Murder," a vital clue establishing the long-disputed identity of a notorious criminal is found in a spooky antique shop in London. Excitement mounts and author Bloch provides a most unusual ending.

Lael Littke's tale, "The Bantam Phantom," gives us an intimate glimpse into the private lives of some very funny spooks. You may shed tears of laughter as you observe how they fare in various human abodes.

Strange and weird things happen to the mailman in "Not Snow Nor Rain," the frightening tale by Miriam Allen deFord. Neither the legendary Persian couriers nor the fierce letter-carriers of Genghis Khan could have shown more courage and tenacity than this United States mailman did on his last appointed round.

"The Dance of the Thirteen Skeletons," by Jack Prelutsky, is an unusual gem of a danse macabre. For maximum enjoyment, you may want to read it aloud.

On his way home, Charley gets lost in New York's Grand Central Station's maze of long corridors and finds himself on an unusual platform. Jack Finney will tell you a great deal more about this strange platform in his fantastic tale, "The Third Level."

"The Monster of Poot Holler," by Ida Chittum, is a very scary tale about two brave young boys who venture into a forbidding marshy ravine. Their perilous adventure will cause sweat to drip from every pore.

The other stories offered in this book are equally enthralling. While you witness all the spooky and frightening goings-on, enjoy every chilling minute of it!

Helen Hoke

NOT SNOW NOR RAIN

Miriam Allen deFord

On his first day as a mail carrier, Sam Wilson noted that inscription, cribbed from Herodotus, on the General Post Office, and took it to heart: "Not snow, nor rain, nor heat, nor gloom of night stays these couriers from the swift completion of their appointed rounds."

It couldn't be literally true, of course. Given a real blizzard, it would be impossible to make his way through the pathless drifts; and if there had been a major flood, he could hardly have swam to deliver letters to the marooned. Moreover, if he couldn't find the addressee, there was nothing to do but mark the envelope "Not known at this address," and take it back to be returned to the addresser or consigned to the Dead Letter Office. But through the years, Sam Wilson had been as consciously faithful and efficient as any Persian messenger.

Now the long years had galloped by, and this was the very last time he would walk his route before his retirement.

It would be good to put his feet up somewhere and ease them back into comfort; they had been Sam's loyal servants and they were more worn out than he was. But the thought of retirement bothered him. Mollie was going to get sick of having him around the house all day, and he was damned if he was going to sit on a park bench like other discarded old men and suck a pipe and stare at nothing, waiting for the hours to pass in a vacuum. He had his big interest, of course— his status as a devoted science fiction fan; he would have time now to read and reread, to watch hopefully from the roof of his apartment house for signs of a flying saucer. But that wasn't enough; what he needed was a project to keep him alert and occupied.

On his last delivery he found it.

The Ochterlonie Building, way down on lower Second Avenue, was a rundown, shabby old firetrap, once as solid as the Scotsman who had built it and named it for himself. But now, with its single open-cage elevator and its sagging floors, it attracted only quack doctors and dubious private eyes and similar fauna on the edge of free enterprise. Sam had been delivering to it now for thirty-five years, watching its slow deterioration.

This time there was a whole batch of self-addressed letters for a tenant whose name was new to him, but that was hardly surprising—nowadays, in the Ochterlonie Building, tenants came and went.

They were small envelopes, addressed in blue, in printing simulating handwriting, to Orville K. Hesterson, Sec.-Treas., Time-Between-Time, 746 Ochterlonie Building, New York, N.Y. 10003. Feeling them with experienced fingers, Sam Wilson judged they were orders for something, doubtless enclosing money.

In most of the buildings on his last route, Sam knew, at least by sight, the employees who took in the mail, and they knew him. A lot of them knew this was his last trip; there were farewells and good wishes, and even a few small donations (since he wouldn't be there next Christmas) which he gratefully tucked in an inside pocket of the uniform he would never wear again. There were also two or three invitations to a drink, which, being still on duty, he had regretfully to decline.

But in the Ochterlonie Building, with its fly-by-night clientele, he was just the postman, and nobody greeted him except Howie Mallory, the decrepit elevator operator. Sam considered him soberly. It was going to be pretty tough financially from now on; could he, perhaps, find a job like Howie's? No. Not unless things got a lot tougher; standing all day would be just as bad as walking.

He went from office to office, getting rid of his load—mostly bills, duns and complaints, he imagined, in this hole. There was nothing for the seventh floor except this bunch for the Time-Between-Time.

The seventh floor? He must be nuts. The Ochterlonie Building was only six floors high.

Puzzled, he rang for Howie.

"What'd they do, build a penthouse office on top of this old dump?" he inquired.

The elevator operator laughed, as at a feeble jest. "Sure," he said airily. "General Motors is using it as a hideaway."

"No, Howie—no fooling. Look here."

Mallory stared and shook his head. "There ain't no 746. Somebody got the number wrong. Or they got the building wrong. And there's nobody here by that name."

"They couldn't—printed envelopes like these."

"O.K., wise guy," said Howie. "Look for yourself."

He led the way to the short flight of iron stairs and the trapdoor. While Mallory stood jeering at him, Sam determinedly climbed through. There was nothing in sight but the plain flat roof. He climbed down again.

"Last letters on my last delivery and I can't deliver them," Sam Wilson said disgustedly.

"Somebody's playing a joke, maybe."

"Crazy joke. Well, so long, Howie. Some young squirt will be taking his life in his hands in this broken-down cage of yours tomorrow."

Sam Wilson, whom nothing could deter from the swift completion of his appointed rounds, had to trudge back to the post office with twenty-two undelivered letters.

Years ago the United States Post Office gave up searching directories and reference books, or deciphering illiterate or screwy addresses, so as to make every possible delivery. That went out with three daily and two Saturday deliveries, two-cent drop postage, and all the other amenities that a submissive public let itself lose without a protest. But there was still a city directory in the office. Sam Wilson searched it stubbornly. Time-Between-Time was not listed. Neither was Orville K. Hesterson.

There was nothing to do but consider the letters "nixies" and turn them over to the proper department. If there was another bunch of them tomorrow, he would never know.

Retirement, after the first carefree week, was just as bad as Sam Wilson had suspected it was going to be. Not bad enough to think yet about elevator operating or night watching, but bad enough to make him restless and edgy, and to make him snap Mollie's head off until they had their first bad quarrel in years. He'd never had time enough before to keep up with all the science fiction magazines and books. Now, with nothing but time, there weren't enough of them to fill the long days. What he needed was something—something that didn't involve walking—to make those endless hours speed up. He began thinking again about those twenty-two "nixies."

He sat gloomily on a bench in Tompkins Square in the spring sunshine: just what he had sworn not to do, but if he stayed home another hour, Mollie would heave the vacuum cleaner at him. In the Public Library he had searched directories and phone books, for all the boroughs and for suburban New Jersey, Connecticut and Pennsylvania; Orville K. Hesterson appeared in none of them.

He didn't know why it was any of his business, except that Time-Between-Time had put a blot on the very end of his thirty-five-year record and he wanted revenge. Also, it was something to do and be interested in. In a way, science fiction and detection had a lot in common, and Sam Wilson prided himself on his ability to guess ahead what was going to happen in a story. So why couldn't he figure out this puzzle, right here in Manhattan, Terra? But he was stymied.

Or was he?

Sam took his gloomy thoughts to Mulligan's. Every large city is a collection of villages. The people who live long enough in a neighborhood acquire their own groceries, their own drugstores, their own bars. The Wilsons had lived six years in their flat, and Mulligan's, cater-cornered across the street, was Sam's personal bar.

He was cautious as to what he said there. He'd heard enough back talk already when he had been indiscreet enough once, after four beers, to express his views on UFOs. He had no desire to gain a reputation as a crackpot. But it was safe enough to remark conversationally. "How do you find out where a guy is when he says he's someplace and you write him there and the letter comes back?"

"*You* ought to know, Sam," said Ed, the day barkeeper. "You were a postman long enough."

"If I knew, I wouldn't ask."

"Ask Information on the phone."

"He hasn't got a phone." That was the weirdest part of it—a business office without a phone.

In every bar, at every moment, there is somebody who knows all the answers. This somebody, a nondescript fellow nursing a Collins, spoke up. "It could be unlisted."

Sam's acquaintances didn't include people with unlisted phones; he hadn't thought of that.

"Then how do you find out his number?"

"You don't, unless he tells you. That's why he has it unlisted."

The police could get it, Sam thought. But they wouldn't, without a reason.

"Hey, maybe this guy's office is in one of them flying saucers and he forgot to come down and get his mail," Ed suggested brightly.

Sam scowled and walked out.

Nevertheless...

Nothing to do with UFOs, of course. That was ridiculous.

But suppose there was a warp in the space-time continuum? Suppose there had once been another Ochterlonie Building, or some day in the future there was going to be another one, somewhere in New York? There wasn't another now, in any of the boroughs, or any other building with a name remotely like it; his research had already established that.

Sam went back to the Public Library. The building, he knew, had been erected in 1898. He consulted directories as far back as they went; there never had been one of the name before. Then a time-slip from the future?

That was hopeless, so far as he could do anything about it, so he cast about for another solution. How about a parallel world?

That could be, certainly: some accident by which mail for that other Ochterlonie Building, the seven-story one, had (maybe just once) arrived in the wrong dimension.

He couldn't do anything to prove or disprove that, either. What he needed was a break.

He got it.

One morning in early summer his own mailbox in the downstairs hallway disgorged a long envelope, addressed to Mr. Samuel Wilson. The upper left-hand corner bore a printed return address: Time-Between-Time, 746 Ochterlonie Building, New York, N.Y. 10003. He raced upstairs, locked himself in the bathroom, the one place Mollie couldn't interrupt him, and tore the envelope open with trembling fingers.

It was a form letter, with the "Dear Mr. Wilson" not too accurately typed in. It enclosed one of those blue-printed envelopes in simulated handwriting. The letterhead carried the familiar impossible address, but no phone number.

Maybe it was chance, maybe it was ESP, but he himself had got onto Time-Between-Time's mailing list!

He had trouble focusing his eyes to read the letter.

Dear Mr. Wilson:

Would you invest $1 to get a chance at $1,000?

Of course you would, especially if, win or lose, you got your dollar back.

In this atomic age, yesterday's science fiction has become today's and tomorrow's science fact. Time-Between-Time, a new organization, is planning the establishment of a publishing company to bring out the best in new books, both fact and fiction, in the field of science, appealing to people who have never been interested until now.

Before we start, we are conducting a poll to find out what the general public thinks and feels about our probabilities of success. We're asking for your cooperation.

Our statisticians have told us that from the answers to one question—which may look off the beam but isn't—we can make a pretty good estimate. Here it is:

If tomorrow morning a spaceship landed in front of your house, and from it issued a band of extra-terrestrial beings, who might or might not be human in appearance, what, in your best judgment, would be your own immediate reaction? Check one, or if you agree with none of the choices, indicate in the blank space beneath what your personal reaction would probably be.

1. Phone for the police. 2. Attack the aliens physically. 3. Faint. 4. Run away. 5. Call for assistance

to seize the visitors. 6. Greet them, attempt to communicate, and welcome them in the name of your fellow-terrestrials. 7. Other (please specify).

Return this letter, properly marked, in the enclosed envelope. To defray promotion expenses, enclose a dollar bill (no checks or money orders).

At the conclusion of this poll, all answers will be evaluated. The writer of the one which comes nearest to the answer reached by our electronic computer, which will be fed the same question, will receive $1,000 in dollar bills. Ties will receive duplicate prizes.

In addition, all participants, when our publishing firm has been established, will receive for their $1 a credit form entitling them to $1 off any book we publish.

Don't delay. Send in your answer NOW. Only letters enclosing $1 will be entered.

> Very truly yours,
> Time-Between-Time,
> *Orville K. Hesterson,*
> Sec.-Treas.

Sam Wilson read the letter three times. "It's crazy," he muttered. "It's a gyp."

What he ought to do was take the letter to the post office—Mr. Gross would be the one to see—and let them decide whether this Hesterson was using the mails to defraud. Let Mr. Gross and his department try to find 746 in the six-story Ochterlonie Building. As a faithful employee for thirty-five years, it was Sam's plain duty.

But then it would be out of his hands forever; he'd never even find out what happened. And he'd be back in the dull morass that retirement was turning out to be.

"Sam!" Mollie yelled outside the locked door. "Aren't you ever coming out of there?"

"I'm coming, I'm coming!" He put the letter and its enclosure back in the envelope and placed them in a pocket.

Time enough to decide that afternoon what he was going to do.

He escaped after lunch to what was becoming his refuge, on a park bench. There he read the letter for the fourth time. For a long while he sat ruminating. About three o'clock he walked to the General Post Office—walking had become a habit hard to break—and hunted up the man who now had his old route, a youngster not more than thirty named Flanagan.

From the letter Sam extracted the return envelope.

"You been delivering any like this?" he asked.

Flanagan peered at it.

"Yeah," he said. "Plenty." He looked worried. "Gee, Wilson, I'm glad you came in. There's something funny about those deliveries, and I don't want to get in Dutch."

"Funny how?"

"My very first day on the route, I started up to the seventh floor of that building to deliver them and there wasn't any seventh floor. So I asked the old elevator man———"

"Howie Mallory. I know him. He's been there for years."

"I guess so. Anyway, he said it was O.K. just to give them to him. He showed me a paper, signed with the name of this outfit, by the secretary or something———"

"Orville K. Hesterson," Sam said.

"That was it—saying that all mail for them was to be delivered to the elevator operator until further notice. So I've been giving it to him ever since. There's a big bunch every day. Is something wrong, Sam? Have I pulled a boner? Am I going to be in trouble?"

"No trouble. I'm just checking—little job they asked me to do for them, seeing I'm retired." Sam was surprised at the glibness with which that fib came out.

Flanagan still looked worried. "He said their office was being remodeled or something, so he was looking after their mail till they could move in."

"Sure. Don't give it another thought." Another idea occurred to him; he lowered his voice. "I oughtn't to tell you this, Flanagan, but every new man on a route, they kind of check up on him the first few weeks, see if he's handling everything O.K. I'll tell them you're doing fine."

"Hey, thanks. Thanks a lot."

"Don't say anything about this. It's supposed to be secret."

"Oh, I won't."

Sam Wilson waved and walked out. He sat on the steps awhile to think.

Was old Howie Mallory pulling a fast one? Was *he* Orville K. Hesterson? Had he cooked up a scheme to make himself some crooked money?

Three things against that. First, those "nixies" the first day: why wouldn't Mallory have told him the same thing he told Flanagan? Sam would have believed him, if he had said they were building an office on the roof and giving it a number.

Second, Howie just wasn't smart enough. Of course he could be fronting for the real crook. But Sam had known him for years, and old Howie had always seemed downright stupidly honest. A man doesn't suddenly turn into a criminal after a lifetime of probity.

Third, if this was some fraudulent scheme involving Mallory, nobody the old man knew, least of all the postman who used to deliver mail to that very building, would ever have been allowed to appear on the sucker list.

Sam Wilson thought some more. Then he hunted up the nearest pay phone and called Mollie.

"Mollie? Sam. Look, I just met an old friend of mine———" He picked a name from a billboard visible from the phone booth————"Bill Seagram, you remember him. Oh, sure you do; you've just forgotten. Anyway, he's just here for the day and we're going to have dinner and see a show. Don't wait up for me. I might be pretty late. No, I'm *not* phoning from Mullings. Now you know me, Mollie; do I ever drink too much? Yeah, sure, he ought to've asked you too, but he didn't. O.K., he's impolite. Aw, Mollie, don't be like that————"

She hung up on him.

Sam Wilson stood concealed in a doorway from which he could see the cramped lobby of the Ochterlonie Building. It was ten minutes before somebody entered it and rang for the elevator. The minute Howie Mallory started up with his passenger, Sam darted into the building and started climbing the stairs. He heard Mallory passing him, going down again, but the elevator wasn't visible from the stairway. On the sixth floor, after a quick survey to see that the hall was clear and the doors closed that he had to pass, he found the iron steps to the trapdoor.

The roof was just as empty as the other time he had visited it. No, it wasn't. In a corner by the parapet, weighted with a brick to keep it from blowing away, was a large paper bag. Sam picked up the brick and looked inside. It was stuffed with those blue-printed envelopes.

He looked carefully about him. There were buildings all around, towering over the little old Ochterlonie Building. There were plenty of windows from which a curious eye could discern anything happening on that roof. But at night anybody in those buildings would be either working late or cleaning offices, with no reason whatever to go to a window; and Sam was sure nothing was going to happen till after dark.

It was a warm day and he had been carrying his coat. He folded it and put it down near the paper bag and sat on it with his back against the parapet. He cursed himself for not having had more foresight; he should have brought something to eat and something to read. Well, he wasn't going to climb down all those stairs and up again. He lit his pipe and began waiting.

He must have dozed off, for he came to himself with a start and found it was almost dark. The paper bag was still there. It was just as well he had slept; now he'd have no trouble staying awake and watching. He might very well be there all night—in fact, he'd have to be, whether anything happened or not. The front door would be locked by now. Mollie would have a fit, but he had his alibi ready.

There was only one explanation left. Not time travel. Not alternate universes. Not an ordinary confidence game. Not—decidedly not—a hoax.

If he was wrong, then tomorrow morning he'd take the whole business to Mr. Gross. But he had a hunch he wasn't going to be wrong.

It was 12:15 A.M. by his wristwatch when he saw it coming.

It had no lights; nobody could have spotted it as it appeared suddenly out of nowhere and climbed straight down. It landed lightly as a drop of dew. The port opened and a small, spare man, very neatly dressed, as Sam could see with eyes accustomed to the darkness, stepped out. Orville K. Hesterson in person.

He tiptoed quickly to the paper bag. Then he saw Sam and stopped short. Sam reached out and grabbed a wrist. It felt like flesh, but he couldn't be sure.

"Who are you? What are you doing here?" the newcomer said in a strained whisper, just like a scared character in a soap opera. So he spoke English. Good. Sam didn't speak anything else.

"I'm from the United States Post Office," Sam replied suavely. (Well, he had been, long enough, hadn't he?)

"Oh. Well, now look, my friend———"

"*You* look. Talk. How much are you paying the elevator operator to put your mail up here every day?"

"Five dollars a day, in dollar bills, six days a week, left in the empty bag," answered Hesterson—it must be Hesterson—sullenly. "That's no crime, is it? Call this my office, and call that my rent. All I need an office for is to have somewhere to get my letters."

"Letters with money in them."

"We have to have funds for postage, don't we?"

"What about the postage on the first mailing list, before you got any dollars to pay for stamps?"

If it had been a little lighter, Sam would have been surer of the alarm that crossed Hesterson's face.

"I—well, we had to fabricate some of your currency for that. We regretted it—we aim to obey all local rules and regulations. As soon as we have enough coming in, we intend to send the amount to the New York postmaster as anonymous conscience money."

"How about the $1,000 prize? And those dollar book credits?"

"Oh, that. Well, we say 'when our publishing firm has been established' don't we? That publishing thing is just a gimmick. As for the $1,000, we give no intimation of when the poll will end."

Sam tightened his grasp on the wrist, which was beginning to wriggle.

"I see. O.K., explain the whole setup. It sounds crazy to me."

"I couldn't agree with you more," said Mr. Hesterson, to Sam's surprise. "That's exactly what, in our own idiom, I told..." Sam couldn't get the name; it sounded like a grunt. "But he's the boss and I'm only a scout, third-class." His voice grew plaintive. "You can't imagine what an ordeal it is, almost every week, to have to land in a secluded place where I can hide the flyer, make my way to New York, and buy a bunch of stamps and mail a batch of letters in broad daylight. We can simulate your paper and printing and typing well enough, but"—that grunt again—"insists we use genuine stamps. I told you we try to follow all your laws, as far as we possibly can. It's very difficult for me to keep this absurd shape for long at one time; I'm exhausted after every trip. I can assure you, these little night excursions from the mother-ship to pick up the letters are the very least of my burdens!"

"What in time does your boss think he's going to gain by such a screwy come-on?"

"'In time'? Oh, just an idiomatic phrase. Like our calling our organization Time-Between-Time, time of course being just a dimension of space. I learned your tongue mostly from the B.B.C. and I don't always understand your speech in New York. My dear sir, do you here on this planet ask your bosses why they concoct their plans? Mine has a very profound mind; that's why he is the boss. All I know is that he persuaded the Council to try it out. A softening-up process—isn't that what you people call it when you use it in your silly wars with one another?"

"Softening for what?" But Sam Wilson knew the answer already.

"Why, for the invasion, of course," said Orville K. Hesterson, whose own real name was probably a grunt. "Surely you must be aware that, with planetwide devastation likely and even imminent, every world whose inhabitants can live comfortably under extreme radiation is looking to yours— Earth, as you call it—as a possible area for colonization? So many planets are so terribly overcrowded—there's always a rush for a new frontier. We've missed out too often; this time we're determined to be first."

"I'll be darned," said Sam, "if I can see how that questionnaire would be of any help to you."

"But it's elementary, as I believe one of your famous law enforcers once declared. First of all, we're gaining a pretty good idea of what kind of reception we're likely to meet when we arrive, and therefore whether we're going to need weapons to destroy what will be left of the population, or can reasonably expect to take over without difficulty. We figure that a cross-section of one of your largest cities will be a pretty good indication, and we can extrapolate from that. In the second place, the question itself is deliberately worded to startle the recipients, who have never in their lives contemplated such a thing as an extraterrestrial visitor————"

"Not me. I'm a science fiction fan from way back. It's all old stuff to me."

Hesterson clicked his tongue, or at least the tongue he was wearing. "Oh, dear, that *was* an error. We tried particularly not to include on our lists subscribers to any of your speculative periodicals. That wasn't my mistake, thank goodness; it was another scout who had the horrible job of spending several days here to compile the lists. Under your present low radioactivity it's real agony for us."

"I'll tell you one mistake you did make, though," said Sam angrily. "You ought to've arranged with the elevator man before your first lot of answers was due. If you want to know, that's how I got onto the whole thing. I'm a mail carrier—I'm retired now, but I was one then—and I was the one supposed to deliver the first batch. Mallory—that's the elevator operator—laughed in my face and told me there wasn't any 746 in this building, and I had to take the letters back to the post office—on my *last* delivery!" Sam couldn't keep the bitterness out of his voice. "After thirty-five years—well, that's neither here nor there. But I didn't like that and I made up my mind to find out what was happening."

"So that's it. Oh, dear, dear. I'll have to compensate for that or I *will* be in trouble."

Sam had had enough. "You are in trouble right now," he growled, pushing the little alien back against the parapet. "We're staying right here till morning, and then I'm going to call for help and take you and your flying saucer or whatever it is straight to the F.B.I."

The counterfeit Mr. Hesterson laughed.

"Oh, no indeed you aren't," he said mildly. "I can slip right back into my own shape whenever I want to—the only reason I haven't done it yet is that then I wouldn't have the equipment to talk to you—and I assure you that you couldn't hold me then. On the contrary. As you just pointed out to me, I did make one bad error, and my boss doesn't like errors. I have no intention of making another one by leaving you here to spread the news."

"What do you mean?" Sam Wilson cried. For the first time, after the years of accustomedness to the idea of extra-terrestrial beings, a thrill of pure terror shot through him.

"This," said the outsider softly.

Before Sam could take another breath, the wrist he was hold-ing slid from his grasp, all of Mr. Hesterson slithered into something utterly beyond imagining, and Sam found himself enveloped in invisible chains against which he was unable to make the slightest struggle. He felt himself being lifted and thrown into the cockpit. Something landed on top of him, undoubtedly the package of prize entries and dollar bills. His last conscious thought was a despairing one of Mollie.

Sam Wilson, devoted mail carrier, was making a longer trip than any Persian courier ever dreamed of, and not snow, nor rain, nor heat, nor gloom of night could stay him from his appointed round.

But he may not be gone forever. If he can be kept alive on that planet in some other solar system, they plan to bring him back as Exhibit One, whenever World War III has made Earth sufficiently radioactive for Orville K. Hesterson's co-planetarians to live here comfortably.

LODGING
FOR THE NIGHT

Joan Aiken

"This sewing machine will last you over sixty years without needing repair or maintenance," said Henry Dulge. He took a quick look at the housewife; that should see her well into her hundred and twenties, he thought. "It is rustless, foolproof, perfectly insulated, five pounds down, and a hundred and forty-eight payments of ninety-nine and a half. I'll leave it with you for a week's trial, shall I? Or will you sign right away? Here's the form...."

"It's ever so kind of you," she said faintly. "But in your advertisement that I saw it said—what I wrote up for was—"

"And of course that entitles you to free service and repair for the first two months, not that you are going to need that with an O-Sew-matic, ha ha!"

"You did say in your advertisement that you had reconditioned models for sale for eight pounds," she persisted timidly.

His face changed. "Oh, well, of course, if you want *that* sort of stuff—We did have just a few, but they're trash, let me assure you, madam, trash! Why, you'd only use one for a few days before you'd be begging me to change it for an O-Sew-matic. Now, this lovely model here, you can make all your children's clothes on it, curtains, quilts, it's like a dream to handle—"

"Haven't you one of the eight-pound models in your van that I could just look at?" she pleaded.

He hesitated. But it was pouring rain, and she looked the sort that could be browbeaten—a pale, pulpy little woman with hair like tangled raffia. "No, I haven't, as a matter of fact," he snapped. "Sold the last one to a silly old fool who didn't know a bad bargain when she saw one. Now you be sensible, madam, you take my advice, you'll never regret it—"

She wavered. "Well—I do want to get on with my husband's winter shirts—"

He handed her the pen.

At this critical moment her husband came home, beer-flavored and hungry for his supper.

"What the blazes is going on here?" he growled, taking in the whole situation—the poised pen, the form with its mass of small print, the seductive glitter of the O-Sew-matic, and Henry Dulge's truculence suddenly turned ingratiating.

"I was just explaining to your good lady here—"

She gave her husband an alarmed, pleading smile, but he was wasting no time.

"Out! And take your flaming machine with you. I'll have no never-never in my house. *Out!*"

The rain blattered against the front window. Henry Dulge was not a coward. He rallied for a last try—but the husband moved towards him so threateningly that he abandoned the hope, picked up the O-Sew-matic, said, with an angry, pitying laugh, "Well, I'm afraid you're going to be very, very sorry for this, madam. You won't often get the chance of such a bargain," and departed, letting the wind slam the door behind him.

Rain sluiced over the aluminium cover of the O-Sew-matic, and he had to rub it dry, cursing, before he drove off into the drenching dusk. He was so annoyed at having missed what promised to be an easy sale that instead of finding a hotel for the night, as he had intended, he drove straight through the town and on along the coast road towards Crowbridge.

The rain spun down in his headlights, thick as thatch, and bounced off the shingle-spattered road. Every half mile or so illuminated signs by the roadside warned: THIS ROAD IMPASSABLE DURING SPRING TIDES WHEN TIDE IS HIGH.

Dulge had no notion whether the tide was at spring or neap, but in any case it was satisfactorily far out—only occasionally when the road curved up over a bluff did he catch a glimpse of tossing, menacing whitecaps, far to his right.

He passed a solitary, plodding walker, a tramp, to judge from his pack and ragged coat, and took a mean pleasure in cutting close past the man to spray him with mud and sand from the wheels. The fellow must be soaked through, anyway; a bit extra wouldn't make much odds.

Ten miles farther on he overtook another pedestrian, this time a girl. She was wearing a dark rain cape but the headlights picked out the white kerchief over her hair. Henry's chivalry came to the fore, and he pulled over beside her and opened the door.

"Hop in, mermaid," he said jovially. She seemed startled, but thanked him, and settled quietly beside him. He let out the clutch, pleased with such a piece of luck: this girl was a peach, a real contest winner, looked a bit chilled with the wet and cold—what the devil was she doing walking along the coast road at this time of night?—but a topnotch figure, what he could see of it, and classy too, with that pale-gold hair trained back from a high forehead.

"Dangerous along here, didn't you know?" he said. "Wouldn't want the tide to come in and wash away a pretty girl like you."

"Oh, I often walk this way," she said carelessly. "There is no danger if you know the state of the tide."

"Live in Crowbridge?"

"Yes, I have a house there."

"All on your own?"

She nodded. His eyes widened. This seemed an unbelievably promising situation.

"That makes two of us then. Here's me, a poor bachelor, don't know a soul in the town. How about cheering me up? Have dinner with me at the Ship?"

"You are kind," she said, "but I never eat at inns."

"How about inviting me round to your place then? Take pity on the stranger, eh?"

She looked at him oddly. "I never invite guests. Those who wish for my hospitality must find the way themselves."

They had entered the small port of Crowbridge and were climbing the main street towards the upper town. Street lamps, wildly swinging from their brackets, threw shifting gleams of light on Tudor gables and brickwork.

"I won't be shy in finding the way, darling, believe me. What's your name? Where's your house?"

"I live near here," she said, "if you will be so kind as to put me down."

"Ah, come on now, darling. At least have a quick one with me at the old Ship, to keep out the wet."

"Thank you no, I—"

But he drove on. He was forced to stop, though, at the traffic lights, and to his annoyance she somehow managed to slip out—heaven knew how she did it, for he thought he had locked the door and that catch was the devil to shift anyway. Before he could let out a word or curse she was gone, following the flutter of her kerchief into the dark rainy night. The lights changed to green, and a furious hooting from behind forced him on, damning her wholeheartedly. But Crowbridge was a small town; maybe someone at the pub would know who she was.

He made straight for the bar and had three doubles in quick succession to sink the memory of the missed sale and the mislaid pickup. Then he inquired about a bed for the night.

"Sorry, sir. I'm afraid we're full right up."

"Full up? In October? Are you crazy?"

"It's the annual conference of the NAFFU, sir. Always held in Crowbridge. I'm afraid you won't find a bed in the town. I know for a fact they're full at the Crown and the George, we've had people come on from there."

"For Pete's sake! Isn't there anywhere in the town I can get a bed—digs, boardinghouse, anything?" He appealed to the other drinkers in the bar. "Can't any of you gentlemen suggest somewhere? It's thirty miles on to Castlegate."

They hesitated. "The road's flooded, too, between here and Castlegate," put in the barman. "I doubt you'd get through that way."

"Well," said one man after a pause, "he could sleep at the old Dormer House."

"What's that?" Henry's hopes rose. "A hostel?"

"No, it's a private house. As a matter of fact it's empty now—due for demolition. Work starts tomorrow. The Council's been itching to get it out of the way for years, but they couldn't touch it till the last of the family died, which she did a couple of months back—an old lady of ninety-three. Historic sort of place. Some society's been protesting about the demolition, but the house sticks right out into a crossroads. Makes a very dangerous corner."

"Ah, well, some of these old places have to come down; can't keep 'em all," Henry agreed. "But I can't stay there if it's empty, can I? I don't fancy sleeping on bare boards."

"Ah, you see, that's the point. It's a kind of celebrated house, the old Dormer—you're sure you haven't heard of it?"

"No, never."

"There's a tradition that if anyone asks to stay, the family will allow them to—Hardisty, the family name was, belonged to the Hardistys since the first Queen Elizabeth's time—and give them free fire and bedding. A clause in the old lady's will, the Miss Hardisty who just died, said this custom was to be kept up till demolition began. So you'll find fires and beds there."

"Free fire and bedding? Sounds too good to be true! Maybe my luck's changing. And about time too."

"There's another thing."

"Well?"

"Anyone who stays there till eight o'clock next morning has a right to claim a thousand pounds from the estate."

"A *thousand pounds?* What do you think I am? A sucker?"

But all the men in the bar assured him that this was perfectly true. They were quite serious. Henry, studying the faces, began to believe them.

"But has nobody claimed it yet?"

"Not one. It's haunted, you see."

"Haunted? What by?" Henry looked sceptical. "I'd like to see the ghost that could shift *me* out of a free bed and a thousand quid."

"By one of the family, a girl called Bess Hardisty, who lived in the first Elizabeth's time. The story goes that her young man fell in love with the Queen. He was so dazzled that he went off and forgot Bess, sailed to discover the Indies and never came back. She turned bitter and sour, lived to be very old, and was finally burned as a witch. Since then no one but members of the family can sleep in the house—she gives people terrible dreams."

Henry burst out laughing. "She'll be clever if she can give *me* dreams! Why, it's a cinch. Can you do me dinner here?" he asked the barman.

"Why, yes, sir, we can manage that."

"All right, you give me some dinner, and then tell me where to find this place. By the way," he added, remembering, "can you tell me the name of a girl who lives on her own here, very pretty girl, about twenty-five, pale blond hair?"

"No, sir, I can't say I can call her to mind," said the barman. "But I haven't been here long." The other men shook their heads. Did some of them look at Henry oddly? It was probably his hunger that made him imagine them suddenly pale and remote, as if seen through glass; he would pursue the matter of the girl when he'd had a good dinner.

The Ship dinner was excellent, but the service was slow. It was near closing time when Henry returned to the bar, and by now he was feeling tired. The men who had been there before were gone now, and the barman seemed preoccupied. Why bother about the girl? If she was lost, she was lost, no sense whining over her. He had a couple more drinks fairly fast, put his car in the town car park, and took the direction the barman had given him.

The rain had let up a little, but it was still too dark to see much of the old Dormer House, and he was in no mood to linger. He pushed open the heavy door and climbed the stairs. No electricity, but he had his powerful car torch, and from somewhere above he could see the glow and hear the comfortable crackle of a blazing fire.

A few rooms he looked into were empty, already stripped of their furniture, but, following the firelight, he found a big stately bedroom with a carpet and chairs and a blue silk-hung fourposter. It smelled delicious, of applewood and lavender. Henry dumped his wet case on the carpet with a grunt of content and punched the mattress.

"This certainly beats the old Ship," he said to himself with satisfaction. "I bet Queen Elizabeth never slept on *that*."

Apart from himself, the house seemed empty. He undressed leisurely by the leaping fire, replenished it from a basket of logs, bolted the door, and got into bed. The bed was even warm—you might have thought one of those Elizabethan things—what did they call them?—warming pans, had just been taken out of it.

And when he was more than halfway into the mist of sleep, a pair of warm arms came round his neck and a voice said gently in his ear, "Did you think you weren't going to see me again? I knew you'd find your way here."

"Is that you, darling?" Henry murmured sleepily. "My luck surely has turned. But how did you get in? I could have sworn there was no one in the place."

"I was here already. Don't you see? I live here...."

It was after him. It was gaining on him. A hundred, five hundred people, women mostly, were watching him with hating eyes, cheering it on, and it was plunging along the road behind him, its great wheel letting off blue sparks as it whirled round, the gigantic needle munching steadily towards him, cutting the tar of the road as if it were cheese. Now it was right alongside him and he was paralyzed, unable to stir, and the needle was above him, vibrating, poised for the terrible downward thrust that would pierce from brain to groin, pinning him to the bed like a butterfly—

He woke sweating, screaming, struggling with the bedclothes. Instinctively he turned to seek the comfort of his bedmate, but she was gone. Could he feel something metallic, hard and ice cold among the sheets? He leapt out as if he had found a snake in the bed. The grip of nightmare was still on him and he started pulling on his clothes with frantic, trembling haste, all other considerations lost in the urge to get out of there. He kept glancing haggardly at the ceiling, as if he expected the great bright needle to come plunging through to impale him. The fire burned bright, but he never noticed the portrait on the wall of a pale, gilt-haired girl smiling primly above her ruff; he overlooked the scatter of clothes on a chair, the brocade skirts, the little square-toed shoes with jewelled buckles. He unbolted the door with shaking hands, stumbled down the stairs, and ran for the parked car like a hunted thing. The rain had stopped, but dead leaves like packs of wolves scurried down the street after him and the wind shook and grappled him. Not a soul stirred; it was the dead hour of night.

He found a board across the Castlegate road: FLOODS, IMPASSABLE, and turned back the way he had come, along the coast road to Trowchester. The tide was nearly full now; he could hear the roar of the waves like a thousand sewing machines, and he cast a nervous glance in the rear mirror, half wondering if he would see *It* coming steadily along behind, munching up the miles. What a hell of a dream. He would have to pack in the job if he had many more like that.

When he turned his eyes back to the road ahead, he found the girl sitting in the car beside him.

He gasped something incoherent. His hands shook and slipped on the wheel.

"You didn't think I'd stay behind, did you?" she said. "I'm coming with you. They're pulling my house down tomorrow, I shall have nowhere to live. It was lucky you came to see me tonight. Now I can come and live in *your* house."

"You can't—you can't!" he gabbled. "I've a wife—children—"

He jabbed his foot on the accelerator, and the car swooped up over a bluff, following the old, winding coast road. But on the far side of the bluff there was no road, only the white-capped waves, warring with the dark of the night, grinding like a thousand sewing machines against the shingle bank. His car ran smoothly in among the crests and disappeared.

At about the same time two policemen were interrogating a tramp in the streets of Crowbridge.

"Let's have a look at that pack of yours," one of them said, mistrusting the raggedness of the man and the suspicious weight of the pack.

"I object," the tramp said with dignity. "It's starting to rain again and I don't want my things all wet."

"You'll have to come along to the station then."

He accompanied them without protest. He was a blue-eyed, weatherbeaten man who might have been any age between forty and seventy. His pack, opened at the police station, proved to contain sheets of paper covered with handwriting, and a number of books.

"Russian," whispered one of the constables. "Think he's a spy, sarge?"

"That's Greek, you ignorant thick," said the sergeant, who had been to Crete. "All right, you can go. Be a bit more cooperative another time."

"It's coming down hard now," the tramp said mildly. "I suppose you can't put me up for the night in a cell?"

"Sorry, mate, cells all full up with trade-union members sleeping it off."

"He could go to the Old Dormer," the constable said.

"Where's that?" the tramp asked.

The sergeant said doubtfully, "Well, I suppose it won't do no harm."

They told him how to get there.

It was raining hard again. The tramp made haste to get indoors but then, instead of going upstairs, found the big stone-flagged kitchen with its massive table, and pulled up a chair. He took a piece of paper, a pencil, and a lump of cheese from his pack, and began writing slowly, with many crossings-out, absently taking a bite of cheese from time to time.

About half an hour later he jumped violently, as he suddenly became aware that someone was looking over his shoulder.

"Why don't you come upstairs?" she said. "There's a fire upstairs."

"Blimey, you gave me a start," he said. "I never heard you come in."

"Come up by the fire?" she repeated.

"All right, miss. That's very kind of you. I'll just finish this."

He wrote for another ten minutes, and then followed her up to the room with the fourposter. The bed was smoothly made, the fire leaping. "Nice place," he said, with appreciation, looking round. He sat by the fire.

"Wouldn't you like to go to bed?" she asked.

"Well, thanks, miss, but I'm not sleepy. Had a good kip under a hedge this afternoon. I think I'll read for a bit, unless you feel like a chat."

"That was a sonnet you were writing, wasn't it? Why do you write sonnets?"

"I dunno, really. I just took a fancy to. That's why I'm on the roads. I used to be a seaman, radio technician, till I retired and had me own little business. Then I took this fancy to write sonnets and learn languages. Well, after all, you've only got one life, got to please yourself sometimes, haven't you? So my daughter and son-in-law that I lived with, they got fed up and gave me the push."

"Your own daughter turned you out?" she said, shocked.

"You couldn't blame her, lass, with me not bringing in any money. Matter of fact, I've been happier since then than ever in me life. No worries, got my transistor if ever I feel lonely. Like a bit of music?"

He turned a switch and suddenly the room was filled with sweet, orderly sound.

"Good, isn't it? That's Hamburg. Made the set myself."

"But that is a galliard!" she said, her face lighting up. "We used to dance to it. Like this!"

She rose and began turning and gliding before him, holding up her brocade skirts so that the jewels in her buckled shoes glittered in the firelight.

"Bravo!" he said. "That's as good as Sadlers' Wells!"

"You dance too!" She caught at his hand. "Oh, what a long time it is since I danced!"

"Me, lass? I don't know how. All I ever learned was the two-step."

"I can show you. See how easy it is? The music carries you."

And indeed it did seem that the music was guiding him

through the intricate courtly pattern of the dance. He stepped erectly, and his blue eyes shone at her as she moved and dipped, graceful as a ship under full sail. One dance followed another, and yet he was not tired, or conscious of any incongruity in their dancing together. At last the music ended and she swept him a deep curtsy.

"See," she said, "we have danced so long that dawn is breaking. I never thought to dance again."

"So we have. So we have. And yet I don't feel tired at all."

THE BANTAM PHANTOM

Lael J. Littke

Georgie's size probably had something to do with his getting fired from his job. As a matter of fact, it had everything to do with it. In the Official Rules and Regulations for Ghosting, Chapter 3, Section 17A (1), it states that an aspiring haunter must be of a size befitting the area he expects to haunt, which is only logical. After all, how could a ghost the size of a napkin expect to haunt the Metropolitan Opera House or Yankee Stadium?

Georgie was very small. He was so small that instead of wearing a sheet the size of a double bed—the way Oscar, the head ghost at Mrs. Pomeroy's did—or even the size of a twin bed sheet like the one Gwendolyn, Oscar's wife, wore, Georgie had to wear a tablecloth. And only the size of a bridge table, at that. And even then a good deal of it floated behind him.

Now, as you know, not all ghosts haunt houses. Most of the smaller ones are content with jobs like pushing out the peanuts in a vending machine or popping up the tissues in a Kleenex box. Georgie had several friends who were also too small to haunt houses—they worked in Grand Central Station lockers. They liked their jobs because it gave them a chance to meet all kinds of people.

Georgie, however, had higher ambitions. He didn't know exactly what it was he wanted to do, but he knew it had to be something impressive. Like being a house haunter. In a big house, and the larger the better. A mansion would be fine.

He never would have got the job at Mrs. Pomeroy's Fifth Avenue mansion if John and Marsha, two of the Pomeroy ghosts, hadn't eloped and left Oscar short of help. Georgie showed up the night of Mrs. Pomeroy's annual dinner party and in the confusion was hired without being measured to see if he met the specified minimum requirements.

But because of his hard work and willingness he was allowed to stay on for a whole year. His main assignment was to haunt the small bedroom in the east wing, usually given to children of visiting guests. The truth was, Oscar wasn't entirely satisfied with Georgie's work there since Georgie could not seem to carry on in the true haunting tradition. Instead of putting a good scare into the children by trailing spider webs across their faces or filling the room with hollow laughter in the dismal hours after midnight, Georgie spent his time whispering fanciful tales into their small ears after they had gone to bed. The little back bedroom became a favorite spot with the children and they cherished forever the memory of the delightful hours they spent there, although they were never quite sure what it was that had made the time so pleasant.

It was at Mrs. Pomeroy's that Georgie met Geraldine, a petite little ghost the size of a dish towel, who worked in Mrs. Pomeroy's bedroom haunting one of her shoeboxes. She and Georgie fell in love and were married at a gala party in the furnace room one romantically dark and stormy night.

Georgie probably would have stayed on at Mrs. Pomeroy's forever if he hadn't tried to carry the heavy chain down the front stairs on the night of Mrs. Pomeroy's next annual dinner party, a tremendous affair which always took the entire ghosting staff. Everyone else was so busy that Oscar asked Georgie to carry the chain and follow him down to the dining room. They were planning to drag it across the waxed floors to see what that would do to the guests.

Everything went smoothly enough—even though Georgie was turning a little pink from his exertions—until he tripped. One of the stair-haunting ghosts had swept past, causing a breeze that swirled Georgie's tablecloth around his feet, and down he went. He tried to scream a warning to Oscar, but it was too late. The heavy chain flattened Oscar, knocking him cold. Before he regained consciousness three days later, he had been laundered and used as a bedsheet for two nights. He fired Georgie.

Georgie broke the news to Geraldine gently, since she was expecting a little handkerchief in a few months. She assured Georgie that she had great faith in him and that it wouldn't be long before he found another job, considering his abilities and brains. They bade a tearful farewell to all their friends at Mrs. Pomeroy's, pulled out the nails in the attic where they hung themselves to sleep in the daytime, and set out to look for a new position.

They could always go home to Dullsville, Pennsylvania, Georgie told Geraldine, and help haunt the coal mine in which his father worked. But they both agreed that to return to a poverty zone like Dullsville would be a step backward. Since both of them had become used to the nicer things in life, they would try to find a position in another mansion.

Each day Georgie scanned the want ads in the New York edition of the Ghost Gazette and wrote stacks of letters of application. Geraldine found an easy job accumulating lint under the beds in a small hotel and they were allowed to live there until Georgie could find a job.

For a few weeks Georgie rented himself out as a tablecloth in a restaurant, a position he rather enjoyed although he regarded it as beneath his dignity. He whispered stories to the restaurant clientele while they ate. The place became a favorite eatery, especially with the arty set. However, when Georgie noticed that he was becoming somewhat threadbare from the constant bleachings, he left that job and worked for a while haunting a TV set in a wonderful dark gloomy little place in Greenwich Village. He wisely quit when he heard the lady of the house phoning a TV repairman to come and get rid of the ghost in her set.

Georgie drifted about for several weeks doing nothing much except calling at the ghost employment office each day to see if anyone had offered him a job. Dispiritedly he tried applying at some of the swanky apartments on Sutton Place, but was usually greeted with hoots of laughter and remarks such as "Who needs a bantam phantom?"

Then one day there was a letter asking him to call at the home of Don Surly, the famous writer of children's stories. Georgie was elated until he found that the job was merely haunting a broom closet. But he hid his disappointment and took it. Geraldine was expecting her handkerchief just about any day and he couldn't afford to be choosy.

It can't be said that Georgie liked his new job, but he did it to the best of his ability. He was told to rattle the mop bucket and moan whenever the maid opened the closet door. Georgie discovered, however, that the maid, an elderly Finn, was practically deaf and noticed neither the rattling nor his moans. To add to his chagrin at being ignored, the maid snatched him one day, tore him in two, and used both halves of him to sop up the scrub water when she washed the floor.

Georgie was so depressed that while Geraldine patched him up, in the cozy cubbyhole they had been assigned to under the stairs, he told her he was ready to go back to Dullsville and haunt the coal mine. It was either that or be a rag mop the rest of his life. In true wifely fashion Geraldine said that wherever he went she would go since she was willing to put up with anything herself, even a coal mine; but, she added sweetly, she wanted something better for their coming little one and certainly wanted it to have all the comforts to be found in a big city. Georgie sighed and decided to stick it out.

It was while he was on his way back to the broom closet that he heard a human voice, a loud male human voice.

"I can't go on," it was saying. "Nothing comes. I sit and stare at this dratted typewriter but my head is empty. I can't write any more."

Georgie heard gentler tones, soothing female tones. He followed the direction of the voices and slipped behind a door. Mr. Surly was striding furiously up and down his den, a booklined room dominated by a large desk on which sat an electric typewriter. Strewn about the desk were piles of crumpled paper.

"I'm drained dry," wailed Mr. Surly. "Empty. I can't conjure up a single fresh idea. I'm a writer who can't write any more. I think I shall kill myself."

"You don't mean that," said Mrs. Surly. "Give yourself a chance to rest and to fill up again with ideas."

"That isn't the way it works!" shouted Mr. Surly. "It's been three months since I wrote a saleable story. I'm a failure, I tell you. We'll have to move out of here."

Oh, oh, thought Georgie, here's where I lose another job. He wondered if Geraldine could stand another move at this delicate time.

Mr. Surly stopped pacing and stared glumly out of the window. "I'll sell shoes," he said. "Or pump gas."

"If that was what you really wanted to do, dear," said Mrs. Surly, "I'd say all right, sell shoes or pump gas—if it were only the two of us to consider. But there are Billy and Walter and Peter and Polly and Edgar and Alice and Randy and Elizabeth and Peggy and Arthur and Jane."

Mr. Surly paled. *"That* many?"

Mrs. Surly nodded. She held up a little bootee she was in the process of knitting.

"Good lord," whispered Mr. Surly. He sat down at the

typewriter. "I am going to write a story today or I shall blow my brains out. At least you and the kids would have the insurance."

"Don't talk like that, dear," said Mrs. Surly.

"Go away. I've got to work." Mr. Surly sat down at the typewriter and scowled ferociously at it as Mrs. Surly tiptoed out.

Georgie crept over and hung around Mr. Surly's shoulder to see what he had been writing. It was a children's story about a garbage truck that murdered a mini-car because the dragon that lived inside the truck told him to do it.

"That's not much of a children's story," whispered Georgie.

"Actually it's *not* much of a children's story," said Mr. Surly to himself.

Georgie leaned closer. "The garbage truck could be an unfortunate ugly old man who is suspected of violence only because he looks like a criminal."

"And the mini-car could be a rich playboy. By George," chortled Mr. Surly, "that's the first good idea I've had for months. I knew *something* would come if I kept at it long enough."

Georgie pondered a moment and then leaned even closer to Mr. Surly's ear. "Actually it was the butler who committed the murder because he was jealous. The ugly old man looks mean but he is really a kind and generous man who is good to his wife. Dogs and children love him."

"Originality, that's what they want," said Mr. Surly. Gaily he began to type.

Georgie stayed right there with him for several hours until the manuscript was finished. He didn't even mind when Mr. Surly reached around and grabbed one of Georgie's corners, thinking it was his handkerchief, and mopped his perspiring face. Georgie regarded it as an honor.

Finally Mr. Surly pulled the last sheet from his typewriter.

"Selma," he bellowed, "I'm a writer again. Come and read this story."

Georgie slipped out while Mrs. Surly was telling Mr. Surly how wonderful he was and that she had known all along he could do it.

"Geraldine," Georgie yelled as he floated home, "I've found out what I'm meant to be."

Geraldine met him at the door of their cubbyhole. "What's the matter?" she said anxiously. "Did your stitches come loose?"

"I've found my niche," sang Georgie. "Geraldine, I'm going to be a ghost writer!"

"Darling, that's wonderful," Geraldine said. "I'm sure you'll be a great success."

And he is, even though only he and Geraldine know that Mr. Surly gets the ideas for all his fine stories—the mysteries, the romances, the adventure and science-fiction stories—from Georgie.

Georgie especially likes doing stories about people who persevere.

MOUSE

Fredric Brown

Bill Wheeler was, as it happened, looking out of the window of his bachelor apartment on the fifth floor, on the corner of 83rd Street and Central Park West, when the spaceship from Somewhere landed. It floated gently down out of the sky and came to rest in Central Park on the open grass between the Simon Bolivar Monument and the walk, barely a hundred yards from Bill Wheeler's window.

Bill Wheeler's hand paused in stroking the soft fur of the Siamese cat lying on the windowsill and he said wonderingly, "What's that, Beautiful?" but the Siamese cat didn't answer. She stopped purring, though, when Bill stopped stroking her. She must have felt something different in Bill—possibly from the sudden rigidness in his fingers or possibly because cats are prescient and feel changes of mood. Anyway she rolled over on her back and said, "Miaouw," quite plaintively. But Bill, for once, didn't answer her. He was too engrossed in the incredible thing across the street in the park.

It was cigar-shaped, about seven feet long and two feet in diameter at the thickest point. As far as size was concerned, it might have been a large toy model dirigible, but it never occurred to Bill—even at his first glimpse of it when it was about fifty feet in the air, just opposite his window—that it might be a toy or a model.

There was something about it, even at the most casual look, that said *alien*. You couldn't put your finger on what it was. Anyway, alien or terrestrial, it had no visible means of support, no wings, propellers, rocket tubes or anything else— and it was made of metal and obviously heavier than air.

But it floated down like a feather to a point just about a foot above the grass. It stopped there and suddenly, out of one end of it (both ends were so nearly alike that you couldn't say it was the front or back) came a flash of fire that was almost blinding. There was a hissing sound with the flash, and the cat, under Bill Wheeler's hand, turned over and was on her feet in a single lithe movement, looking out of the window. She spat once, softly, and the hair on her back and the back of her neck stood straight up, as did her tail, which was now a full two inches thick.

Bill didn't touch her; if you know cats, you don't when they're like that. But he said, "Quiet, Beautiful. It's all right. It's only a spaceship from Mars, to conquer Earth. It isn't a mouse."

He was right on the first count, in a way. He was wrong on the second, in a way. But let's not get ahead of ourselves like that.

After the single blast from its exhaust tube, or whatever it was, the spaceship dropped the last twelve inches and lay inert on the grass. It didn't move. There was now a fan-shaped area of blackened earth radiating from one end of it, for a distance of about thirty feet.

And then nothing happened except that people came running from several directions. Cops came running too, three of them, and kept people from going too close to the alien object. Too close, according to the cops' idea, seemed to be not closer than about ten feet. Which, Bill Wheeler thought, was silly. If the thing was going to explode or anything, it would probably kill everyone for blocks around.

But it didn't explode. It just lay there, and nothing happened. Nothing except that flash that had startled both Bill and the cat. And the cat looked bored now, and lay back down on the windowsill, her hackles down.

Bill stroked her sleek fawn-colored fur again, absentmindedly. He said, "This is a day, Beautiful. That thing out there is from *outside,* or I'm a spider's nephew. I'm going down and take a look at it."

He took the elevator down. He got as far as the front door, tried to open it and couldn't. All he could see through the glass were the backs of people, jammed tight against the door. Standing on tiptoes and stretching his neck to see over the nearest ones, he could see a solid phalanx of heads stretching from here to there.

He got back in the elevator. The operator said, "Sounds like excitement out front. Parade going by or something?"

"Something," Bill said. "Spaceship just landed in Central Park from Mars or somewhere. You hear the welcoming committee out there."

"The hell," said the operator. "What's it doing?"

"Nothing."

The operator grinned. "You're a great kidder, Mr. Wheeler. How's that cat you got?"

"Fine," said Bill. "How's yours?"

"Getting crankier. Threw a book at me when I got home last night with a few under my belt and lectured me half the night because I'd spent three and a-half bucks. You got the best kind."

"I think so," Bill said.

By the time he got back to the window, there was really a crowd down there. Central Park West was solid with people for half a block each way and the park was solid with them for a long way back. The only open area was a circle around the spaceship, now expanded to about twenty feet in radius, and with a lot of cops keeping it open, instead of only three.

Bill Wheeler gently moved the Siamese over to one side of the windowsill and sat down. He said, "We got a box seat, Beautiful. I should have had more sense than to go down there."

The cops below were having a tough time. But reinforcements were coming, truckloads of them. They fought their way into the circle and then helped enlarge it. Somebody had obviously decided that the larger that circle was, the fewer people were going to be killed. A few khaki uniforms had infiltrated the circle, too.

"Brass," Bill told the cat. "High brass. I can't make out insignia from here, but that one boy's at least a three-star; you can tell by the way he walks."

They got the circle pushed back to the sidewalk, finally. There was a lot of brass inside by then. And half a dozen men, some in uniform, some not, were starting very carefully, to work on the ship. Photographs first, and then measurements, and then one man with a big suitcase of paraphernalia was carefully scratching at the metal and making tests of some kind.

"A metallurgist, Beautiful," Bill Wheeler explained to the Siamese, who wasn't watching at all. "And I'll bet you ten pounds of liver to one miaouw he finds that's an alloy that's brand new to him. And that it's got some stuff in it he can't identify.

"You really ought to be looking out, Beautiful, instead of lying there like a dope. This is a *day*, Beautiful. This may be the beginning of the end—or of something new. I wish they'd hurry up and get it open."

Army trucks were coming into the circle now. Half a dozen big planes were circling overhead, making a lot of noise. Bill looked up at them quizzically.

"Bombers, I'll bet, with pay loads. Don't know what they have in mind, unless to bomb the park, people and all, if little green men come out of that thing with ray guns and start killing everybody. Then the bombers could finish off whoever's left."

But no little green men came out of the cylinder. The men working on it couldn't apparently, find an opening in it. They'd rolled it over now and exposed the underside, but the underside was the same as the top. For all they could tell, the underside *was* the top.

And then Bill Wheeler swore. The army trucks were being unloaded, and sections of a big tent were coming out of them, and men in khaki were driving stakes and unrolling canvas.

"They *would* do something like that, Beautiful," Bill complained bitterly. "Be bad enough if they hauled it off, but to leave it there to work on and still to block off our view————"

The tent went up. Bill Wheeler watched the top of the tent, but nothing happened to the top of the tent and whatever went on inside he couldn't see. Trucks came and went, high brass and civvies came and went.

And after a while the phone rang. Bill gave a last affectionate rumple to the cat's fur and went to answer it.

"Bill Wheeler?" the receiver asked. "This is General Kelly speaking. Your name has been given to me as a competent research biologist. Tops in your field. Is that correct?"

"Well," Bill said. "I'm a research biologist. It would be hardly modest for me to say I'm tops in my field. What's up?"

"A spaceship has just landed in Central Park."

"You don't say," said Bill.

"I'm calling from the field of operations; we've run phones in here, and we're gathering specialists. We would like you and some other biologists to examine something that was found inside the—uh—spaceship. Grimm of Harvard was in town and will be here and Winslow of New York University is already here. It's opposite 83rd Street. How long would it take you to get here?"

"About ten seconds, if I had a parachute. I've been watching you out of my window." He gave the address and the apartment number. "If you can spare a couple of strong boys in imposing uniforms to get me through the crowd, it'll be quicker than if I try it myself. Okay?"

"Right. Send 'em right over. Sit tight."

"Good," said Bill. "*What* did you find inside the cylinder?"

There was a second's hesitation. Then the voice said, "Wait till you get here."

"I've got instruments," Bill said. "Dissecting equipment. Chemicals. Reagents. I want to know what to bring. Is it a little green man?"

"No," said the voice. After a second's hesitation again, it said, "It seems to be a mouse. A dead mouse."

"Thanks," said Bill. He put down the receiver and walked back to the window. He looked at the cat accusingly. "Beautiful," he demanded, "was somebody ribbing me, or————"

There was a puzzled frown on his face as he watched the scene across the street. Two policemen came hurrying out of the tent and headed directly for the entrance of his apartment building. They began to work their way through the crowd.

"Fan me with a blowtorch, Beautiful," Bill said. "It's the McCoy." He went to the closet and grabbed a valise, hurried to a cabinet and began to stuff instruments and bottles into the valise. He was ready by the time there was a knock on the door.

He said, "Hold the fort, Beautiful. Got to see a man about a mouse." He joined the policemen waiting outside his door and was escorted through the crowd and into the circle of the elect and into the tent.

There was a crowd around the spot where the cylinder lay. Bill peered over shoulders and saw that the cylinder was neatly split in half. The inside was hollow and padded with something that looked like fine leather, but softer. A man kneeling at one end of it was talking.

"Not a trace of any activating mechanism, any mechanism at *all*, in fact. Not a wire, not a grain or a drop of any fuel. Just a hollow cylinder, padded inside. Gentlemen, it *couldn't* have traveled by its own power in any conceivable way. But it came here, and from outside. Gravesend says the material is definitely extraterrestrial. Gentlemen, I'm stumped."

Another voice said, "I've an idea, Major." It was the voice of the man over whose shoulder Bill Wheeler was leaning and Bill recognized the voice and the man with a start. It was the Governor of New York. Bill quit leaning on him.

"I'm no scientist," the Governor said. "And this is just a possibility. Remember the one blast, out of that single exhaust hole? That might have been the destruction, the dissipation of whatever the mechanism or the propellant was. Whoever, whatever, sent or guided this contraption might not have wanted us to find out what made it run. It was constructed, in that case, so that upon landing, the mechanism destroyed itself utterly. Colonel Roberts, you examined the scorched area of ground. Anything that might bear out that theory?"

"Definitely, sir," said another voice. "Traces of metal and silica and some carbon, as though it had been vaporized by terrific heat and then condensed and uniformly spread. You can't find a chunk of it to pick up, but the instruments indicate it. Another thing———"

Someone tapped Bill Wheeler on the shoulder. "You're Wheeler, aren't you?"

Bill turned. "Professor Winslow!" he said. "I've seen your picture, sir, and I've read your papers in the Journal. I'm proud to meet you and to———"

"Cut the malarkey," said Professor Winslow, "and take

a gander at this." He grabbed Bill Wheeler by the arm and led him to a table in one corner of the tent.

"Looks for all the world like a dead mouse," he said, "but it isn't. Not quite. I haven't cut in yet; waited for you and Grimm. But I've taken temperature tests and had hairs under the mike and studied musculature. It's—well, look for yourself."

Bill Wheeler looked. It looked like a mouse all right, a very small mouse, until you looked closely. Then you saw little differences, if you were a biologist.

Grimm got there and—delicately, reverently—they cut in. The differences stopped being little ones and became big ones. The bones didn't seem to be made of bone, for one thing, and they were bright yellow instead of white. The digestive system wasn't too far off the beam, and there was a circulatory system and a white milky fluid in it, but there wasn't any heart. There were instead, nodes at regular intervals along the larger tubes.

"Way stations," Grimm said. "No central pump. You might call it a lot of little hearts instead of one big one. Efficient, I'd say. Creature built like this couldn't have heart trouble. Here, let me put some of that white fluid on a slide."

Someone was leaning over Bill's shoulder, putting uncomfortable weight on him. He turned his head to tell the man to get the hell away and saw it was the Governor of New York. "Out of this world?" the Governor asked quietly.

"And how," said Bill. A second later he added, "Sir," and the Governor chuckled. He asked, "Would you say it's been dead long or that it died about the time of arrival?"

Winslow answered that one. "It's purely a guess because we don't know the chemical make-up of the thing, or what its normal temperature is. But a rectal thermometer reading twenty minutes ago, when I got here, was ninty-five point three, and one minute ago it was ninty point six. At that rate of heat loss, it couldn't have been dead long."

"Would you say it was an intelligent creature?"

"I wouldn't say for sure, Sir. It's too alien. But I'd guess—definitely no. No more so than its terrestrial counterpart, a mouse. Brain size and convolutions are quite similar."

"You don't think it could, conceivably, have designed that ship?"

"I'd bet a million to one against it, Sir."

It had been mid-afternoon when the spaceship had landed; it was almost midnight when Bill Wheeler started home. Not from across the street, but from the lab at New York University, where the dissection and microscopic examinations had continued.

He walked home in a daze, but he remembered guiltily that the Siamese hadn't been fed, and hurried as much as he could for the last block.

She looked at him reproachfully and said, "Miaouw, miaouw, miaouw, miaouw..." so fast he couldn't get a word in edgewise until she was eating some liver he took out of the icebox.

"Sorry, Beautiful," he said then. "Sorry, too, I couldn't bring you that mouse, but they wouldn't have let me if I'd asked and I didn't ask because it would probably have given you indigestion."

He was still so excited that he couldn't sleep that night. When it got early enough he hurried out for the morning papers to see if there had been any new discoveries or developments.

There hadn't been. There was less in the papers than he knew already. But it was a big story and the papers played it big.

He spent most of three days at the New York U. lab, helping with further tests and examinations until there just weren't any new ones to try and darn little left to try them on. Then the government took over what was left and Bill Wheeler was on the outside again.

For three more days he stayed home, tuned in to all news reports on the radio and video and read every newspaper published in English in New York City. But the story gradually died down. Nothing further happened; no further discoveries were made and if any new ideas developed, they weren't given out for public consumption.

It was on the sixth day that an even bigger story broke— the assassination of the president of the United States. People forgot the spaceship.

Two days later the prime minister of Great Britain was killed by a Spaniard and the day after that a minor employee of the Politburo in Moscow ran amok and shot a very important official.

A lot of windows broke in New York City the next day, when a goodly portion of a county in Pennsylvania went up fast and came down slowly. No one within several hundred miles needed to be told that there was—or had been—a dump of A-bombs there. It was in sparsely populated country and not many people were killed, only a few thousand.

That was the afternoon, too, that the president of the Stock Exchange cut his throat and the crash started. Nobody paid too much attention to the riot at Lake Success the next day because of the unidentified submarine fleet that suddenly sank practically all the shipping in New Orleans harbor.

It was the evening of that day that Bill Wheeler was pacing up and down the front room of his apartment. Occasionally he stopped at the window to pet the Siamese named Beautiful and to look out across Central Park, bright under lights and cordoned off by armed sentries, where they were pouring concrete for the anti-aircraft gun emplacements.

He looked haggard.

He said, "Beautiful, we saw the start of it, right from this window. Maybe I'm crazy, but I still think that spaceship started it. God knows how. Maybe I should have fed you that mouse. Things couldn't have gone to pot so *suddenly* without help from somebody or something."

He shook his head slowly. "Let's dope it out, Beautiful. Let's say something came in on that ship besides a dead mouse. What *could* it have been? What could it have done and be doing?"

"Let's say that the mouse was a laboratory animal, a guinea pig. It was sent in the ship and it survived the journey but died when it got here. Why? I've got a screwy hunch, Beautiful."

He sat down in a chair and leaned back, staring up at the ceiling. He said, "Suppose the superior intelligence—from Somewhere—that made that ship, came in with it. Suppose it wasn't the mouse—let's call it a mouse. Then, since the mouse was the only physical thing in the spaceship, the being, the invader, wasn't physical. It was an entity that could live apart from whatever body it had, back where it came from. But let's say it could live in *any* body and it left its own in a safe place back home and rode here in one that was expendable, that it could abandon on arrival. That would explain the mouse and the fact that it died at the time the ship landed.

"Then, the *being,* at that instant, just jumped into the body of someone here—probably one of the first people to run toward the ship when it landed. It's living in somebody's body—in a hotel on Broadway or a flophouse on the Bowery or anywhere—pretending to be a human being. That make sense, Beautiful?"

He got up and started to pace again.

"And having the ability to control other minds, it sets about to make the world—the Earth—safe for Martians or Venusians or whatever they are. It sees—after a few days of study—that the world is on the brink of destroying itself and needs only a push. So it could give that push."

"It could get inside a nut and make him assassinate the President, and get caught at it. It could make a Russian shoot his Number One. It could make a Spaniard shoot the Prime Minister of England. It could start a bloody riot in the United Nations, and make an army man, there to guard it, explode an A-bomb dump. It could—hell, Beautiful, it could push this world into a final war within a week. It practically *has* done it."

He walked over to the window and stroked the cat's sleek fur while he frowned at the gun emplacements going up under the bright floodlights.

"And he's done it, and even if my guess is right I couldn't stop him because I couldn't find him. And nobody would believe me, now. He'll make the world safe for Martians. When the war is over, a lot of little ships like that—or big ones—can land here and take over what's left ten times as easy as they could now."

He lighted a cigarette, with hands that shook a little. He said, "The more I think of it, the more———"

He sat down in the chair again. He said, "Beautiful, I've got to *try*. Screwy as that idea is, I've got to give it to the authorities, whether they believe it or not. That Major I met was an intelligent guy. So is General Kelly. I———"

He started to walk to the phone and then sat down again. "I'll call both of them, but let's work it out just a little finer first. See if I can make any intelligent suggestions how they could go about finding the—the *being*."

He groaned. "Beautiful, it's impossible. It wouldn't even have to be a human being. It could be an animal, anything. It could even be *you*. He'd probably take over whatever nearby type of mind was nearest his own. If he was remotely feline, you'd have been the nearest cat."

He sat up and stared at her. He said, "I'm going crazy, Beautiful. I'm remembering how you jumped and twisted just after that spaceship blew up its mechanism and went inert. And, listen, Beautiful, you've been sleeping twice as much as usual lately. Has your mind been out————"

"Say, *that* would be why I couldn't wake you up yesterday to feed you, Beautiful. Cats always wake up easily. *Cats* do."

Looking dazed, Bill Wheeler got up out of the chair. He said, "Cat, *am* I crazy, or————"

The Siamese cat looked at him languidly through sleepy eyes. Distinctly it said, *"Forget it."*

And halfway between sitting and rising, Bill Wheeler looked even more dazed for a second. He shook his head as though to clear it.

He said, "What was I talking about, Beautiful? I'm punchy from not enough sleep."

He walked over to the window and stared out, gloomily, rubbing the cat's fur until it purred.

He said, "Hungry, Beautiful? Want some liver?"

The cat jumped down from the windowsill and rubbed itself against his leg affectionately.

It said, *"Miaouw."*

ONLY
A DREAM

Sir Henry Rider Haggard

Footprints—footprints—the footprints of one dead. How ghastly they look as they fall before me! Up and down the long hall they go, and I follow them. *Pit, pat* they fall, those unearthly steps, and beneath them starts up that awful impress. I can see it grow upon the marble, a damp and dreadful thing.

Tread them down, tread them out; follow after them with muddy shoes, and cover them up. In vain. See how they rise through the mire! Who can tread out the footprints of the dead?

And so on, up and down the dim vista of the past, following the sound of the dead feet that wander so restlessly, stamping on the impress that will not be stamped out. Rave on, wild wind, eternal voice of human misery; fall, dead footsteps, eternal echo of human memory; stamp, miry feet; stamp into forgetfulness that which will not be forgotten.

And so on, on to the end.

Pretty indeed, these for a man about to be married, especially when they float into his brain at night like ominous clouds into a summer sky, and he is going to be married tomorrow. There is no mistake about it—the wedding, I mean. To be plain and matter-of-fact, why there stand the presents, or some of them, and very handsome presents they are, ranged in solemn rows upon the long table. It is a remarkable thing to observe, when one is about to make a really satisfactory marriage, how scores of unsuspected or forgotten friends crop up and send little tokens of their esteem. It was very different when I married my first wife, I remember, but then that marriage was not satisfactory—just a love-match, no more.

There they stand in solemn rows, as I have said, and inspire me with beautiful thoughts about the innate kindness of human nature, especially the human nature of our distant cousins. It is possible to grow almost poetical over a silver teapot when one is going to be married tomorrow. On how many future mornings shall I be confronted with that teapot? Probably for all my life; and on the other side of the teapot will be the cream jug, and the electroplated urn will hiss away behind them both. Also the sugar basin will be in front, full of sugar, and behind everything will be my second wife.

"My dear," she will say, "will you have another cup of tea?" and probably I shall have another cup.

Well, it is very curious to notice what ideas will come into a man's head sometimes. Sometimes, something waves a magic wand over his being, and from the recesses of his soul dim things arise and walk. At unexpected moments they come, and he grows aware of the issues of his mysterious life, and his heart shakes and shivers like a lightning-shattered tree. In that dreary light all earthly things seem far, and all unseen things draw near and take shape and awe him, and he knows not what is true and what is false; neither can he trace the edge that marks off the Spirit from the Life. Then it is that the footsteps echo, and the ghostly footprints will not be stamped out.

Pretty thoughts again! and how persistently they come! It is one o'clock and I will go to bed. The rain is falling in sheets outside. I can hear it lashing against the window panes, and the wind wails through the tall, wet elms at the end of the garden. I could tell the voice of those elms anywhere; I know it as well as the voice of a friend. What a night it is! We sometimes get them in this part of England in October. It was just such a night when my first wife died, and that is three years ago. I remember how she sat up in bed.

"Ah! Those horrible elms," she said. "I wish you would have them cut down, Frank; they cry like a woman." And I said I would, and just after that she died, poor dear. And so the old elms stand, and I like their music. It is a strange thing; I was half-brokenhearted, for I loved her dearly, and she loved me with all her life and strength, and now—I am going to be married again.

"Frank, Frank, don't forget me!" Those were my wife's last words; and, indeed, though I am going to be married again tomorrow, I have not forgotten her. Nor shall I forget how Annie Guthrie (whom I am going to marry now) came to see her the day before she died. I know that Annie always liked me, more or less, and I think that my dear wife guessed it. After she had kissed Annie and bid her a last good-bye, and the door had closed, she spoke quite suddenly: "There goes your future wife, Frank," she said. "You should have married her at first instead of me; she is very handsome and very good, and she has two thousand a year; *she* would never have died of a nervous illness." And she laughed a little, and then added, "Oh, Frank dear, I wonder if you will think of me before you marry Annie Guthrie. Wherever I am I shall be thinking of you."

And now that time which she foresaw has come, and Heaven knows that I have thought of her, poor dear. Ah! Those footsteps of one dead that will echo through our lives, those woman's footprints on the marble flooring which will not be stamped out. Most of us have heard and seen them at some time or other, and I hear and see them very plainly tonight. Poor dead wife, I wonder if there are any doors, in the land where you have gone through, which you can creep out of to look at me tonight? I hope that there are none. Death must indeed be hell if the dead can see and feel and take measure of the forgetful faithlessness of their beloved. Well, I will go to bed and try to get a little rest. I am not so young or so strong as I was, and this wedding wears me out. I wish that the whole thing were done or had never been begun.

What was that? It was not the wind, for it never makes that sound here, and it was not the rain, since the rain has ceased its surging for a moment, nor was it the howling of a dog for I keep none. It was more like the crying of a woman's voice but what woman can be abroad on such a night or at such an hour—half-past one in the morning?

There it is again—a dreadful sound; it makes the blood turn chill, and yet has something familiar about it. It is a woman's voice calling around the house. There, she is at the window now, and rattling it, and great heavens! She is calling me.

"Frank! Frank! Frank!" she calls.

I strive to stir and unshutter that window, but before I can get there she is knocking and calling at another.

Gone again, with her dreadful wail of "Frank! Frank!" Now I hear her at the front door, and, half-mad with a horrible fear, I run down the long, dark hall and unbar it. There is nothing there—nothing but the wild rush of the wind and the drip of rain from the portico. But I hear the wailing voice going around the house, past the patch of shrubbery. I close the door and listen. There, she has gone through the little yard, and is at the back door now. Whoever it is, she must know the way about the house. Along the hall I go again, through a swing door, through the servants' hall, stumbling down some steps into the kitchen, where the embers of the fire are still alive in the grate, diffusing a little warmth and light into the dense gloom.

Whoever it is at the door is knocking now with her clenched hand against the hard wood, and it is wonderful, though she knocks so low, how the sound echoes through the empty kitchen.

There I stood and hesitated, trembling in every limb; I dared not open the door. No words of mine can convey the sense of utter desolation that overpowered me. I felt as though I were the only living man in the whole world.

"*Frank! Frank!*" cries the voice with the dreadful familiar ring in it. "Open the door; I am so cold. I have so little time."

My heart stood still, and yet my hands were constrained to obey. Slowly, slowly I lifted the latch and unbarred the door, and, as I did so, a great rush of air snatched it from my hands and swept it wide. The black clouds had broken a little overhead, and there was a patch of blue, rain-washed sky with just a star or two glimmering in it fitfully. For a moment I could only see this bit of sky, but by degrees I made out the accustomed outline of the great trees swinging furiously against it, and the rigid line of the coping of the garden wall beneath them. Then a whirling leaf hit me smartly on the face, and instinctively I dropped my eyes onto something that as yet I could not distinguish—something small and black and wet.

"What are you?" I gasped. Somehow I seemed to feel that it was not a person—I could not say, *who* are you?

"Don't you know me?" wailed the voice, with the far-off familiar ring about it. "And I cannot come in and show myself. I haven't the time. You were so long opening the door, Frank, and I am so cold—oh, so bitterly cold! Look there, the moon is coming out, and you will be able to see me. I suppose that you long to see me, as I have longed to see you."

As the figure spoke, or rather wailed, a moonbeam struggled through the watery air and fell on it. It was short and shrunken, the figure of a tiny woman. Also it was dressed in black and wore a black covering over the whole head, shrouding it, after the fashion of a bridal veil. From every part of this veil and dress, the water fell in heavy drops.

The figure bore a small basket on her left arm, and her hand—such a poor, thin little hand—gleamed white in the moonlight. I noticed that on the third finger was a red line, showing that a wedding ring had once been there. The other hand was stretched towards me as though in entreaty.

All this I saw in an instant, as it were, and as I saw it, horror seemed to grip me by the throat as though it were a living thing. For as the voice had been familiar, so was the form familiar, though the churchyard had received it long years ago. I could not speak—I could not even move.

"Oh, don't you know me yet?" wailed the voice. "And I have come from so far to see you, and I cannot stop. Look, look," and she began to pluck feverishly with her poor, thin hand at the black veil that enshrouded her. At last it came off, and, as in a dream, I saw what in a dim frozen way I had expected to see—the white face and pale yellow hair of my dead wife. Unable to speak or to stir, I gazed and gazed. There was no mistake about it, it was she, aye, even as I had last seen her, white with the whiteness of death, with purple circles around her eyes and the gravecloth yet beneath her chin. Only her eyes were wide open and fixed upon my face; and a lock of the soft yellow hair had broken loose, and the wind tossed it.

"You know me *now*, Frank, don't you, Frank? It has been so hard to come to see you, and so cold! But you are going to be married tomorrow, Frank; and I promised—oh, a long time ago—to think of you when you were going to be married, wherever I was, and I have kept my promise, and I have come from where I am and brought a present with me. It was bitter to die so young! I was so young to die and leave you, but I had to go. Take it, take it! Be quick, I cannot stay any longer! *I could not give you my life, Frank, so I have brought you my death—take it!"*

The figure thrust the basket into my hand, and as it did so the rain came up again, and began to obscure the moonlight.

"I must go, I must go," went on the dreadful, familiar voice, in a cry of despair. "Oh, why were you so long opening the door? I wanted to talk to you before you married Annie; and now I shall never see you again. Never! Never! *Never!* I have lost you forever! Ever! Ever!"

As the last wailing notes died away the wind came down with a rush and a whirl and the sweep as of a thousand wings, and threw me back into the house, bringing the door to close with a crash after me.

I staggered into the kitchen, the basket in my hand, and set it on the table. Just then, some embers of the fire fell in, and a faint little flame rose and glimmered on the bright dishes on the dresser, even revealing a tin candlestick, with a box of matches by it. I was well-nigh mad with the darkness and fear, and, seizing the matches, I struck one, and held it to the candle. Presently it caught, and I glanced around the room. It was just as usual, just as the servants had left it, and above the mantelpiece the eight-day clock ticked away solemnly. While I looked at it, it struck two, and in a dim fashion I was thankful for its friendly sound.

Then I looked at the basket. It was of very fine white plaited work with black bands running up it, and a checkered black and white handle. I knew it well. I have never seen another like it. I bought it years ago at Madeira, and gave it to my poor wife. Ultimately it was washed overboard in a gale in the Irish Channel. I remember that it was full of newspapers and library books, and I had to pay for them. Many and many is the time that I have seen that identical basket standing there on that very kitchen table, for my dear wife always used it to put flowers in, and the shortest way from that part of the garden where her roses grew was through the kitchen. She used to gather the flowers, and then come in and place her basket on the table, just where it stood now, and order the dinner.

All this passed through my mind in a few seconds as I stood there with the candle in my hand, feeling indeed half-dead, and yet with my mind painfully alive. I began to wonder if I had gone asleep, and was the victim of a nightmare. No such thing. I wish it had only been a nightmare. A mouse ran out along the dresser and jumped onto the floor, making quite a crash in the silence.

What was in the basket? I feared to look, and yet some power within me forced me to it. I drew near to the table and stood for a moment listening to the sound of my own heart. Them I stretched out my hand and slowly raised the lid of the basket.

"I could not give you my life, so I have brought you my death!" Those were her words. What could she mean—what could it all mean? I must know or I'd go mad. There it lay, whatever it was, wrapped up in linen.

Ah, heaven help me! It was a small bleached human skull!

A dream! After all, only a dream by the fire, but what a dream. And I am to be married tomorrow.

Can I be married tomorrow?

THE DANCE OF THE THIRTEEN SKELETONS

Jack Prelutsky

In a snow-enshrouded graveyard
gripped by winter's bitter chill,
not a single soul is stirring,
all is silent, all is still
till a distant bell tolls midnight
and the spirits work their will.

For emerging from their coffins
buried deep beneath the snow,
thirteen bony apparitions
now commence their spectral show,
and they gather in the moonlight
undulating as they go.

> And they'll dance in their bones,
> in their bare bare bones,
> with the click and the clack
> and the chitter and the chack
> and the clatter and the chatter
> of their bare bare bones.

They shake their flimsy shoulders
and they flex their fleshless knees
and they nod their skulls in greeting
in the penetrating breeze
as they form an eerie circle
near the gnarled and twisted trees.

They link their spindly fingers
as they promenade around
casting otherwordly shadows
on the silver-mantled ground
and their footfalls in the snowdrift
make a soft and susurrous sound.

And they dance in their bones,
in their bare bare bones,
with the click and the clack
and the chitter and the chack
and the clatter and the chatter
of their bare bare bones.

The thirteen grinning skeletons
continue on their way
as to strains of soundless music
they begin to swing and sway
and they circle ever faster
in their ghastly roundelay.

Faster, faster ever faster
and yet faster now they race,
winding, whirling, ever swirling
in the frenzy of their pace
and they shimmer in the moonlight
as they spin themselves through space.

And they dance in their bones,
in their bare bare bones,
with the click and the clack
and the chitter and the chack
and the clatter and chatter
of their bare bare bones.

Then as quickly as it started
their nocturnal dance is done
for the bell that is their signal
loudly tolls the hour of one
and they bow to one another
in their bony unison.

Then they vanish to their coffins
by their ghostly thoroughfare
and the emptiness of silence
once more fills the frosted air
and the snows that mask their footprints
show no sign that they were there.

But they danced in their bones,
in their bare bare bones,
with the click and the clack
and the chitter and the chack
and the clatter and the chatter
of their bare bare bones.

Shadows from the dim hereafter
hang from every creaking rafter,
laughing disembodied laughter
in their ghostly glee.
Shades of evanescent matter
whisper their unearthly patter,
rattle chains that chill and shatter
on their spectral spree.

Revenants on misty perches
taunt the ghost that lunges, lurches
as it desperately searches
for its vanished head.
Shapeless wraiths devoid of feeling
hover blindly by the ceiling
ranting, chanting, shrieking, squealing
promises of dread.

In the corners, eyes are gleaming,
everywhere are nightmares streaming,
diabolic horrors screaming
in the sombrous air.
So shun this place where spectres soar—
it's you and you they're waiting for
to haunt your souls forevermore
in their castle of despair.

THURNLEY ABBEY

Perceval London

Three years ago I was on my way out to the East, and as an extra day in London was of some importance, I took the Friday evening mail train to Brindisi instead of the usual Thursday morning Marseilles express. Many people shrink from the long forty-eight-hour train journey through Europe, and the subsequent rush across the Mediterranean on the nineteen-knot *Isis* or *Osiris;* but there is really very little discomfort on either the train or the mail boat, and unless there is actually nothing for me to do, I always like to save the extra day and a half in London before I say goodbye to her for one of my longer tramps.

This time—it was early, I remember, in the shipping season, probably about the beginning of September—there were few passengers, and I had a compartment in the P. & O. Indian express to myself all the way from Calais. All Sunday I watched the blue waves dimpling the Adriatic, and the pale rosemary along the cuttings; the plain white towns, with their flat roofs and their bold "duomos," and the gray-green olive orchards of Apulia. The journey was just like any other. We ate in the dining car as often and as long as we decently could; we slept after luncheon; we dawdled the afternoon away with yellow-backed novels; sometimes we exchanged platitudes in the smoking room, and it was there that I met Alastair Colvin.

Colvin was a man of middle height, with a resolute, well-cut jaw; his hair was turning gray; his moustache was sun-whitened; otherwise he was clean-shaven—obviously a gentleman, and obviously also a preoccupied man. He had no great wit. When spoken to, he made the usual remarks in the right way, and I dare say he refrained from banalities only because he spoke less than the rest of us; most of the time he buried himself in the Wagon-lit Company's timetable, but seemed unable to concentrate his attention on any one page of it. He found that I had been over the Siberian railway, and for a quarter of an hour he discussed it with me. Then he lost interest in it, and rose to go to his compartment. But he came back again very soon, and seemed glad to pick up the conversation again.

Of course this did not seem to me to be of any importance. Most travelers by train become a trifle infirm of purpose after thirty-six hours' rattling. But Colvin's restless way I noticed in somewhat marked contrast with the man's personal importance and dignity; especially ill-suited was it to his finely-made large hand with strong, broad, regular nails and its few lines. As I looked at his hand I noticed a long, deep, and recent scar of ragged shape. However, it is absurd to pretend that I thought anything was unusual. I went off at five o'clock on Sunday afternoon to sleep away the hour or two that had still to be got through before we arrived at Brindisi.

Once there, we few passengers transshipped our hand baggage, verified our berths—there were only a score of us in all—and then, after an aimless ramble of half an hour in Brindisi, we returned to dinner at the Hotel International, not wholly surprised that the town had been the death of Virgil. If I remember rightly, there is a gaily painted hall at the International—I do not wish to advertise anything, but there is no other place in Brindisi at which to await the coming of the mails—and after dinner I was looking with awe at a trellis overgrown with blue vines, when Colvin moved across the room to my table. He picked up *Il Secolo,* but almost immediately gave up the pretense of reading it. He turned squarely to me and said:

"Would you do me a favor?"

One doesn't do favors to stray acquaintances on Continental expresses without knowing something more of them than I knew of Colvin. But I smiled in a noncommittal way, and asked him what he wanted. I wasn't wrong in part of my estimate of him; he said bluntly:

"Will you let me sleep in your cabin on the *Osiris?*" And he colored a little as he said it.

Now, there is nothing more tiresome than having to put up with a stable-companion at sea, and I asked him rather pointedly:

"But surely there is room for all of us?" I thought that perhaps he had been partnered off with some angry Levantine, and wanted to escape from him at all hazards.

Colvin, still somewhat confused, said: "Yes, I am in a cabin by myself. But you would do me the greatest favor if you would allow me to share yours."

This was all very well, but besides the fact that I always sleep better when alone, there had been some recent thefts on board English liners, and I hesitated, frank and honest and self-conscious as Colvin was. Just then the mail train came in with a clatter and a rush of escaping steam, and I asked him to see me again about it on the boat when we started. He answered me curtly—I suppose he saw the mistrust in my manner—"I am a member of White's." I smiled to myself as he said it, but I remembered in a moment that the man—if he were really what he claimed to be, and I make no doubt that he was—must have been sorely put to it before he urged the fact as a guarantee of his respectability to a total stranger at a Brindisi hotel.

That evening, as we cleared the red and green harbor lights of Brindisi, Colvin explained. This is his story in his own words:

"When I was traveling in India some years ago, I made the acquaintance of a youngish man in the Woods and Forests. We camped out together for a week, and I found him a pleasant companion. John Broughton was a lighthearted soul when off duty, but a steady and capable man in any of the small emergencies that continually arise in that department. He was liked and trusted by the natives, and though a trifle over-pleased with himself when he escaped to civilization at Simla or Calcutta, Broughton's future was well assured in Government service. When a fair-sized estate was unexpectedly left to him, however, he joyfully shook the dust of the Indian plains from his feet and returned to England. For five years he drifted about London. I saw him now and then. We dined together about every eighteen months, and I could trace pretty exactly the gradual sickening of Broughton with a merely idle life. He then set out on a couple of long voyages, returned as restless as before, and at last told me that he had decided to marry and settle down at his place, Thurnley Abbey, which had long been empty. He spoke about looking after the property and standing for his constituency in the usual way. Vivien Wilde, his *fiancee*, had I suppose, begun to take him in hand. She was a pretty girl with a deal of fair hair and rather an exclusive manner; deeply religious in a narrow school, she was still kindly and high-spirited, and I thought that Broughton was in luck. He was quite happy and full of information about his future.

"Among other things, I asked him about Thurnley Abbey. He confessed that he hardly knew the place. The last tenant, a man called Clarke, had lived in one wing for fifteen years and seen no one. He had been a miser and a hermit. It was the rarest thing for a light to be seen at the Abbey after dark. Only the barest necessities of life were ordered, and the tenant himself received them at the side door. His one manservant, after a month's stay in the house, had abruptly left without warning and had returned to the Southern States. One thing Broughton complained bitterly about: Clarke had wilfully spread the rumor among the villagers that the Abbey was haunted, and had even condescended to play childish tricks with spirit lamps and salt in order to scare trespassers away at night. He had been detected in the act of this tomfoolery, but the story spread, and no one, said Broughton, would venture near the house except in broad daylight. The hauntedness of Thurnley Abbey was now, he said with a grin, part of the gospel of the countryside, but he and his young wife were going to change all that. Would I propose myself any time I liked? I, of course, said I would, and equally, of course, intended to do nothing of the sort without a definite invitation.

"The house was put in thorough repair, though not a stick of the old furniture and tapestry was removed. Floors and ceilings were relaid: the roof was made watertight again, and the dust of half a century was scoured out. He showed me some photographs of the place. It was called an Abbey, though as a matter of fact it had been only the infirmary of the long-vanished Abbey of Closter, some five miles away. The larger part of this building remained as it had been in pre-Reformation days, but a wing had been added in Jacobean times, and that part of the house had been kept in something like repair by Mr. Clarke. He had, in both the ground and first floors, set a heavy timber door, strongly barred with iron, in the passage between the earlier and the Jacobean parts of the house, and had entirely neglected the former. So there had been a good deal of work to be done.

"Broughton, whom I saw in London two or three times about this period, made a deal of fun over the positive refusal of the workmen to remain after sundown. Even after the electric light had been put into every room, nothing would induce them to remain, though, as Broughton observed, electric light was death on ghosts. The legend of the Abbey's ghosts had gone far and wide, and the men would take no risks. They went home in batches of five and six, and even during the daylight hours there was an inordinate amount of talking between one and another, if either happened to be out of sight of his companion. On the whole, though nothing of any sort or kind had been conjured up, even by their heated imaginations, during their five month's work upon the Abbey, the belief in ghosts was rather strengthened than otherwise in Thurnley because of the men's confessed nervousness, and local tradition declared itself in favor of the ghost of an immured nun.

'Good old nun!' said Broughton.

"I asked him whether in general he believed in the possibility of ghosts, and rather to my surprise, he said that he couldn't say he entirely disbelieved in them. A man in India had told him one morning in camp that he believed that his mother was dead in England, as her vision had come to his tent the night before. He had not been alarmed, but had said nothing, and the figure vanished again. As a matter of fact, the next possible *dak-walla* brought on a telegram announcing the mother's death. 'There the thing was,' said Broughton. But at Thurnley he was practical enough. He roundly cursed the idiotic selfishness of Clarke, whose silly antics had caused all the inconvenience. At the same time, he couldn't refuse to sympathize to some extent with the ignorant workmen. 'My own idea,' said he, 'is that if a ghost ever does come in one's way, one ought to speak to it.'

"I agreed. Little as I knew of the ghost world and its conventions, I had always remembered that a spook was in honor bound to wait to be spoken to. It didn't seem much to do, and I felt that the sound of one's own voice would at any rate reassure oneself as to one's wakefulness. But there are few ghosts outside Europe—few, that is, that a white man can see—and I had never been troubled with any. However, as I have said, I told Broughton that I agreed.

"So the wedding took place, and I went to it in a tall hat

which I bought for the occasion, and the new Mrs. Broughton smiled very nicely at me afterwards. As it had to happen, I took the Orient Express that evening and was not in England again for nearly six months. Just before I came back I got a letter from Broughton. He asked if I could see him in London or come to Thurnley, as he thought I should be better able to help him than anyone else he knew. His wife sent a nice message to me at the end, so I was reassured about at least one thing. I wrote from Budapest that I would come and see him at Thurnley two days after my arrival in London, and as I sauntered out of the Pannonia into the Kerepesi Utcza to post my letters, I wondered of what earthly service I could be to Broughton. I had been out with him after tiger on foot, and I would imagine few men better able, at a pinch, to manage their own business. However, I had nothing to do, so after dealing with some small accumulations of business during my absence, I packed a kit-bag and departed to Euston.

"I was met by Broughton's great limousine at Thurnley Road Station and after a drive of nearly seven miles we echoed through the sleepy streets of Thurnley village, into which the main gates of the park thrust themselves, splendid with pillars and spread-eagles and tom-cats rampant atop them. I never was a herald, but I know that the Broughtons have the right to supporters—Heaven knows why! From the gate a quadruple avenue of beech trees led inwards for a quarter of a mile. Beneath them a neat strip of fine turf edged the road and ran back until the poison of the dead beech leaves killed it under the trees. There were many wheel tracks on the road, and a comfortable little pony trap jogged past me, laden with a country parson and his wife and daughter. Evidently there was some garden party going on at the Abbey. The road dropped away to the right at the end of the avenue, and I could see the Abbey across a wide pasture and a broad lawn, thickly dotted with guests.

"The end of the building was plain. It must have been almost mercilessly austere when it was first built, but time had crumbled the edges and toned the stone down to an orange-lichened gray wherever it showed behind its curtain of magnolia, jasmine, and ivy. Farther on was the three-storied Jacobean house, tall and handsome. There had not been the slightest attempt to adapt the one to the other, but the kindly ivy had glossed over the touching-point. There was a tall flèche in the middle of the building, surmounting a small bell tower. Behind the house there rose the mountainous verdure of Spanish chestnuts all the way up the hill.

"Broughton had seen me coming from afar, and walked across from his other guests to welcome me before turning me over to the butler's care. This man was sandy-haired and rather inclined to be talkative. He could, however, answer hardly any questions about the house; he had, he said only been there three weeks. Mindful of what Broughton had told me, I made no inquiries about ghosts, though the room into which I was shown might have justified anything. It was a very large low room with oak beams projecting from the white ceiling. Every inch of the walls, including the doors, was covered with tapestry, and a remarkably fine Italian four-post bedstead, heavily draped, added to the darkness and dignity of the place. All the furniture was old, well-made, and dark. Underfoot there was a plain green pile carpet, the only new thing about the room except the electric light fittings and the jugs and basins. Even the looking glass on the dressing table was an old pyramidal Venetian glass set in a heavy repoussé frame of tarnished silver.

"After a few minutes' cleaning up, I went downstairs and out upon the lawn, where I greeted my hostess. The people gathered there were of the usual country type, all anxious to be pleased and roundly curious as to the new master of the Abbey. Rather to my surprise, and quite to my pleasure, I rediscovered Glenham, whom I had known well in old days in Barotseland. He lived quite close, as, he remarked with a grin, I ought to have known. 'But,' he added, 'I don't live in a place like this.' He swept his hand to the long, low lines of the Abbey in obvious admiration, and then, to my intense interest, muttered beneath his breath, 'Thank God!' He saw that I had overheard him, and turning to me said decidedly, 'Yes, "thank God" I said, and I meant it. I wouldn't live in the Abbey for all Broughton's money.'

" 'But surely,' I demurred, 'you know that old Clarke was discovered in the very act of setting light to his bug-a-boos?'

"Glenham shrugged his shoulders. 'Yes, I know about that. But there is something wrong with the place still. All I can say is that Broughton is a different man since he has lived here. I don't believe that he will remain much longer. But—you're staying here?—well, you'll hear all about it tonight. There's a big dinner, I understand.' The conversation turned off to old reminiscences, and Glenham soon after had to go.

"Before I went to dress that evening I had a twenty minutes' talk with Broughton in his library. There was no doubt that the man was altered, gravely altered. He was nervous and fidgety, and I found him looking at me only when my eye was off him. I naturally asked him what he wanted of me. I told him I would do anything I could, but that I couldn't conceive what he lacked that I could provide. He said with a lusterless smile that there was, however, something, and that he would tell me the following morning. It struck me that he was somehow ashamed of himself, and perhaps ashamed of the part he was asking me to play. However, I dismissed the subject from my mind and went up to dress in my palatial room. As I shut the door a draught blew out the Queen of Sheba from the wall, and I noticed that the tapestries were not fastened to the wall at the bottom. I have always held very practical views about spooks, and it has often seemed to me that the slow waving in firelight of loose tapestry upon a wall would account for ninety-nine percent of the stories one hears. Certainly the dignified undulation of this lady with her attendants and huntsmen—one of whom was untidily cutting the throat of a fellow deer upon the very steps on which King Solomon, a gray-faced Flemish nobleman with the order of the Golden Fleece, awaited his fair visitor—gave color to my hypothesis.

"Nothing much happened at dinner. The people were very much like those of the garden party. A young woman next to me seemed anxious to know what was being read in London. As she was far more familiar than I with the most recent magazines and literary supplements, I found salvation in being myself instructed in the tendencies of modern fiction. All true art, she said, was shot through and through with melancholy. How vulgar were the attempts at wit that marked so many modern books! From the beginning of literature it had always been tragedy that embodied the highest attainment of every age. To call such works morbid merely begged the question. No thoughtful man—she looked sternly at me through the steel rim of her glasses—could fail to agree with me. Of course, as one would, I immediately and properly said that I slept with Pett Ridge and Jacobs under my pillow at night, and that if *Jorrocks* weren't quite so large, I would add him to the company. She hadn't read any of them, so I was saved—for a time. But I remember grimly that she said that the dearest wish of her life was to be in some awful and soul-freezing situation of horror, and I remember that she dealt hardly with the hero of Nat Paynter's vampire story, between nibbles at her brown-bread ice. She was a cheerless soul, and I couldn't help thinking that if there were many such in the neighborhood, it was not surprising that Old Glenham had been stuffed with some nonsense or other about the Abbey. Yet nothing could well have been less creepy than the glitter of silver and glass, and the subdued lights and cackle of conversation all around the dinner table.

"After the ladies had gone I found myself talking to the rural dean. He was a thin, earnest man, who at once turned the conversation to old Clarke's buffooneries. But, he said, Mr. Broughton had introduced such a new and cheerful spirit, not only into the Abbey, but, he might say, into the whole

neighborhood, that he had great hopes that the ignorant su-
perstitions of the past were from henceforth destined to ob-
livion. Thereupon his other neighbor, a portly gentleman of
independent means and positions, audibly remarked 'Amen,'
which damped the rural dean, and we talked of partridges
past, partridges present, and pheasants to come. At the other
end of the table Broughton sat with a couple of his friends,
red-faced hunting men. Once I noticed that they were dis-
cussing me, but I paid no attention to it at the time. I remembered it a few hours later.

"By eleven all the guests were gone, and Broughton, his
wife, and I were alone together under the fine plaster ceiling
of the Jacobean drawing room. Mrs. Broughton talked about
one or two of the neighbors, and then, with a smile, said that
she knew I would excuse her, shook hands with me, and
went off to bed. I am not very good at analyzing things, but
I felt that she talked a little uncomfortably and with a suspicion
of effort, smiled rather conventionally, and was obviously
glad to go. These things seem trifling enough to repeat, but
I had throughout, the faint feeling that everything was not
square. Under the circumstances, this was enough to set me
wondering what on earth the service could be that I was to
render—wondering also whether the whole business was not
ill-advised, just in order to make me come down from London
for a mere shooting party.

"Broughton said little after she had gone. But he was
evidently laboring to bring the conversation around to the so-
called haunting of the Abbey. As soon as I saw this, of course
I asked him directly about it. He then seemed at once to lose
interest in the matter. There was no doubt about it: Broughton
was somehow a changed man, and to my mind he had changed
in no way for the better. Mrs. Broughton seemed no sufficient
cause. He was clearly fond of her, and she of him. I reminded
him that he was going to tell me what I could do for him in
the morning, pleaded my journey, lighted a candle, and went

upstairs with him. At the end of the passage leading into the old house he grinned weakly and said, 'Mind, if you see a ghost, do talk to it; you said you would.' He stood irresolutely a moment and then turned away. At the door of his dressing room he paused once more. 'I'm here,' he called out, 'if you should want anything. Good night,' and he shut his door.

"I went along the passage to my room, undressed, switched on a lamp beside my bed, read a few pages of *The Jungle Book,* and then, more than ready for sleep, turned the light off and went fast asleep.

"Three hours later I woke up. There was not a breath of wind outside. There was not even a flicker of light from the fireplace. As I lay there, an ash tinkled slightly as it cooled, but there was hardly a gleam of the dullest red in the grate. An owl cried among the silent Spanish chestnuts on the slope outside. I idly reviewed the events of the day, hoping that I should fall off to sleep again before I reached dinner. But at the end I seemed as wakeful as ever. There was no help for it. I must read my *Jungle Book* again till I felt ready to go off, so I fumbled for the pear at the end of the cord that hung down inside the bed, and I switched on the bedside lamp. The sudden glory dazzled me for a moment. I felt under my pillow for my book with half-shut eyes. Then, growing used to the light, I happened to look down to the foot of my bed.

"I can never tell you really what happened then. Nothing I could ever confess in the most abject words could even faintly picture to you what I felt. I know that my heart stopped dead, and my throat shut automatically. In one instinctive movement I crouched back up against the headboard of the bed, staring at the horror. The movement set my heart going again, and the sweat dripped from every pore. I am not a particularly religious man, but I had always believed that God would never allow any supernatural appearance to present itself to man in such a guise and in such circumstances that harm, either bodily or mental, could result to him. I can only tell you that at that moment both my life and my reason rocked unsteadily on their seats."

The other *Osiris* passengers had gone to bed. Only he and I remained leaning over the starboard railing, which rattled uneasily now and then under the fierce vibration of the over-engined mail boat. Far over, there were the lights of a few fishing smacks riding out the night, and a great rush of white combing and seething water fell out and away from us over-side.

At last Colvin went on:

"Leaning over the foot of my bed, looking at me, was a figure swathed in a rotten and tattered veiling. This shroud passed over the head, but left both eyes and the right side of the face bare. It then followed the line of the arm down to where the hand grasped the bed-end. The face was not entirely that of a skull, though the eyes and the flesh of the face were totally gone. There was a thin, dry skin drawn tightly over the features, and there was some skin left on the hand. One wisp of hair crossed the forehead. It was perfectly still. I looked at it, and it looked at me, and my brains turned dry and hot in my head. I still had the pear of the electric lamp in my hand, and I played idly with it; only I dared not turn the light out again. I shut my eyes, only to open them in a hideous terror the same second. The thing had not moved. My heart was thumping, and the sweat cooled me as it evaporated. Another cinder tinkled in the grate, and a panel creaked in the wall.

"My reason failed me. For twenty minutes, or twenty seconds, I was able to think of nothing but this awful figure, till there came, hurtling through the empty channels of my senses, the remembrance that Broughton and his friends had discussed me furtively at dinner. The dim possibility of its being a hoax stole gratefully into my unhappy mind, and once there, one's pluck came creeping back along a thousand tiny veins. My first sensation was one of blind unreasoning thankfulness that my brain was going to stand the trial. I am not a timid man, but the best of us needs some human handle to steady him in time of extremity, and in the faint but growing hope that after all, it might be only a brutal hoax, I found the fulcrum that I needed. At last I moved.

"How I managed to do it I cannot tell you, but with one spring towards the foot of the bed I got within arm's length and struck out one fearful blow with my fist at the thing. It crumbled under it, and my hand was cut to the bone. With a sickening revulsion after the terror, I dropped half-fainting across the end of the bed. So it was merely a foul trick after all. No doubt the trick had been played many a time before: no doubt Broughton and his friends had had some large bet among themselves as to what I should do when I discovered the gruesome thing. From my state of abject terror I found myself transported into an insensate anger. I shouted curses upon Broughton. I dived rather than climbed over the bed-end onto the sofa. I tore at the robed skeleton—how well the whole thing had been carried out, I thought—I broke the skull against the floor, and stamped upon its dry bones. I flung the head away under the bed and rent the brittle bones of the trunk in pieces. I snapped the thin thighbones across my knee, and flung them in different directions. The shinbones I set up against a stool and broke with my heel. I raged like a Berserker against the loathly thing, and stripped the ribs from the backbone and slung the breastbone against the cupboard. My fury increased as the work of destruction went on. I tore the frail rotten veil into twenty pieces, and the dust went up over everything, over the clean blotting paper and the silver inkstand. At last my work was done. There was but a raffle of broken bones and strips of parchment and crumbling wool. Then, picking up a piece of the skull—it was the cheek and the templebone of the right side, I remember—I opened the door and went down the passage to Broughton's dressing room. I remember still how my sweat-dripping pajamas clung to me as I walked. At the door I kicked and entered.

"Broughton was in bed. He had already turned the light on and seemed shrunken and horrified. For a moment he could hardly pull himself together. Then I spoke; I don't know what I said. Only I know that from a heart full and overfull with hatred and contempt, spurred on by shame of my own recent cowardice, I let my tongue run on. He answered nothing. I was amazed at my own fluency. My hair still clung lankily to my wet temples, my hand was bleeding profusely, and I must have looked a strange sight. Broughton huddled himself up at the head of the bed just as I had. Still he made no answer, no defense. He seemed preoccupied with something besides my reproaches, and once or twice moistened his lips with his tongue. But he could say nothing, though he moved his hands now and then, just as a baby who cannot speak moves its hands.

"At last the door into Mrs. Broughton's room opened and she came in, white and terrified. 'What is it? What is it? Oh, in God's name! What is it?' she cried again and again, and then she went up to her husband and sat on the bed in her nightdress, and the two faced me. I told her what the matter was. I spared her husband not a word for her presence there. Yet he seemed hardly to understand. I told the pair that I had spoiled their cowardly joke for them. Broughton looked up.

"'I have smashed the foul thing into a hundred pieces,' I said. Broughton licked his lips again and his mouth worked. 'By God!' I shouted, 'it would serve you right if I thrashed you within an inch of your life. I will take care that not a decent man or woman of my acquaintance ever speaks to you again. And there,' I added, throwing the broken piece of the skull upon the floor beside his bed, 'there is a souvenir for you, of your damned work tonight!'

"Broughton saw the bone, and in a moment it was his turn to frighten me. He squealed like a hare caught in a trap. He screamed and screamed till Mrs. Broughton, almost as bewildered as myself, held onto him and coaxed him like a child to be quiet. But Broughton—and as he moved I thought that ten minutes ago I perhaps looked as terribly ill as he did—thrust her from him, and scrambled out of bed onto the floor, and still screaming put out his hand to the bone. It had blood on it from my hand. He paid no attention to me whatever. In truth I said nothing. This was a new turn indeed to the horrors of the evening. He rose from the floor with the bone in his hand and stood silent. He seemed to be listening. 'Time, time, perhaps,' he muttered, and almost at the same moment fell at full length on the carpet, cutting his head against the fender. The bone flew from his hand and came to rest near the door. I picked Broughton up, haggard and broken, with blood over his face. He whispered hoarsely and quickly, 'Listen, listen!' We listened.

"After ten seconds' utter quiet, I seemed to hear something. I could not be sure, but at last there was no doubt. There was a quiet sound as of one moving along the passage. Little regular steps came towards us over the hard oak flooring. Broughton moved to where his wife sat, white and speechless, on the bed, and pressed her face into his shoulder.

"Then, the last thing that I could see as he turned the light out, he fell forward with his own head pressed into the pillow of the bed. Something in their company, something in their cowardice, helped me, and I faced the open doorway of the room, which was outlined fairly clearly against the dimly-lighted passage. I put out one hand and touched Mrs. Broughton's shoulder in the darkness. But at the last moment I too failed. I sank on my knees and put my face in the bed. Only we all heard. The footsteps came to the door, and there they stopped. The piece of bone was lying inside the door. There was a rustle of moving stuff, and the thing was in the room. Mrs. Broughton was silent; I could hear Broughton's voice praying, muffled in the pillow; I was cursing my own cowardice. Then the steps moved out again on the oak boards of the passage, and I heard the sounds dying away. In a flash of remorse I went to the door and looked out. At the end of the corridor I thought I saw something that moved away. A moment later the passage was empty. I stood with my forehead against the jamb of the door almost physically sick.

"'You can turn the light on,' I said, and there was an answering flare. There was no bone at my feet. Mrs. Broughton had fainted. Broughton was almost useless, and it took me ten minutes to bring her to. Broughton only said one thing worth remembering. For the most part he went on muttering prayers. But I was glad afterwards to recollect that he had said that thing. He said in a colorless voice, half as a question, half as a reproach, 'You didn't speak to her.'

"We spent the remainder of the night together. Mrs. Broughton actually fell off into a kind of sleep before dawn, but she suffered so horribly in her dreams that I shook her into consciousness again. Never was dawn so long in coming. Three or four times Broughton spoke to himself. Mrs. Broughton would then just tighten her hold on his arm, but she could say nothing. As for me, I can honestly say that I grew worse as the hours passed and the light strengthened. The two violent reactions had battered down my steadiness of view, and I felt that the foundations of my life had been built upon the sand. I said nothing, and after binding up my hand with a towel, I did not move. It was better so. They helped me and I helped them, and we all three knew that our reason had gone very near to ruin that night. At last, when the light came in pretty strongly, and the birds outside were chattering and singing, we felt that we must do something. Yet we never moved. You might have thought that we should particularly dislike being found as we were by the servants: yet nothing of that kind mattered a straw, and an overpowering listlessness bound us as we sat, until Chapman, Broughton's man, actually knocked and opened the door. None of us moved. Broughton, speaking hardly and stiffly, said, 'Chapman, you can come back in five minutes.' Chapman was a discreet man, but it would have made no difference to us if he had carried his news to the 'room' at once.

"We looked at each other and I said I must go back. I meant to wait outside till Chapman returned. I simply dared not reenter my bedroom alone. Broughton roused himself and said that he would come with me. Mrs. Broughton agreed to remain in her own room for five minutes if the blinds were drawn up and all the doors left open.

"So Broughton and I, leaning stiffly one against the other, went down to my room. By the morning light that filtered past the blinds we could see our way, and I released the blinds. There was nothing wrong in the room from end to end, except smears of my own blood on the end of the bed, on the sofa, and on the carpet where I had torn the thing to pieces."

Colvin had finished his story. There was nothing to say. Seven bells stuttered out from the fo'c'sle, and the answering cry wailed through the darkness. I took him downstairs.

"Of course I am much better now, but it is a kindness of you to let me sleep in your cabin."

MONKEYS

E. F. Benson

Dr. Hugh Morris, while still in his early thirties, had justly earned for himself the reputation of being one of the most dexterous and daring surgeons in his profession, and both in his private practice and in his voluntary work at one of the great London hospitals his record of success as an operator was unparalleled among his colleagues. He believed that vivisection was the most fruitful means of progress in the science of surgery. He believed, rightly or wrongly, that he was justified in causing suffering to animals, though sparing them all possible pain, if thereby he could reasonably hope to gain fresh knowledge about similar operations on human beings which would save life or mitigate suffering: the motive was good, and the gain already immense. But he had nothing but scorn for those who, for their own amusement, took out packs of hounds to run foxes to death, or matched two greyhounds to see which would give the death grip to a single terrified hare: that, to him, was wanton torture, utterly unjustifiable. Year in and year out, he took no holiday at all, and for the most part he occupied his leisure, when the day's work was over, in study.

He and his friend Jack Madden were dining together one warm October night at his house looking onto Regent's Park. The windows of his drawing room on the ground floor were open, and they sat smoking, when dinner was done, on the broad window seat. Madden was starting next day for Egypt, where he was engaged in archaeological work, and he had been vainly trying to persuade Morris to join him for a month up the Nile, where he would be engaged throughout the winter in the excavation of a newly discovered cemetery across the river from Luxor, near Medinet Habu. But it was no good.

"When my eye begins to fail and my fingers to falter," said Morris, "it will be time for me to think of taking my ease. What do I want with a holiday? I should be pining to get back to my work all the time. I like work better than loafing. Purely selfish."

"Well, be unselfish for once," said Madden. "Besides, your work would benefit. It can't be good for a man never to relax. Surely freshness is worth something."

"Precious little if you're as strong as I am. I believe in continual concentration if one wants to make progress. One may be tired, but why not? I'm not tired when I'm actually engaged on a dangerous operation, which is what matters. And time's so short. Twenty years from now I shall be past my best, and I'll have my holiday then, and when my holiday is over, I shall fold my hands and go to sleep for ever and ever. Thank God, I've got no fear that there's an afterlife! The spark of vitality that has animated us burns low and then goes out like a wind-blown candle, and as for my body, what do I care what happens to that, when I have done with it? Nothing will survive of me except some small contribution I may have made to surgery, and in a few years time that will be superseded. But for that I perish utterly."

Madden squirted some soda into his glass.

"Well, if you've quite settled that———" he began.

"I haven't settled it, science has," said Morris. "The body is transmuted into other forms; worms batten on it; it helps to feed the grass; and some animal consumes the grass. But as for the survival of the individual spirit of a man, show me one title of scientific evidence to support it. Besides, if it did survive, all the evil and malice in it must surely survive too. Why should the death of the body purge that away? It's a nightmare to contemplate such a thing, and oddly enough, unhinged people like spiritualists want to persuade us, for our consolation, that the nightmare is true. But odder still are those old Egyptians of yours, who thought that there was something sacred about their bodies, after they were quit of them. And didn't you tell me that they covered their coffins with curses on anyone who disturbed their bones?"

"Constantly," said Madden. "It's the general rule in fact. Marrowy curses written in hieroglyphics on the mummy case or carved on the sarcophagus."

"But that's not going to deter you this winter from opening as many tombs as you can find, and rifling from them any objects of interest or value."

Madden laughed. "Certainly it isn't," he said. "I take out of the tombs all objects of art, and I unwind the mummies to find and annex their scarabs and jewelry. But I make an absolute rule always to bury the bodies again. I don't say that I believe in the power of those curses, but anyhow a mummy in a museum is an indecent object."

"But if you found some mummied body with an interesting malfunction, wouldn't you send it to some anatomical institute?" asked Morris.

"It has never happened to me yet," said Madden, "but I'm pretty sure I shouldn't."

"Then you're a superstitious Goth and an antieducational Vandal," remarked Morris. "Hullo, what's that?" He leaned out of the window as he spoke. The light from the room vividly illuminated the square of lawn outside, and across it was crawling the small twitching shape of some animal. Hugh Morris vaulted out of the window, and presently returned, carrying carefully in his spread hands a little gray monkey, evidently desperately injured. Its hind legs were stiff and out-stretched as if it was partially paralyzed.

Morris ran his soft deft fingers over it.

"What's the matter with the little begger, I wonder," he said. "Paralysis of the lower limbs: it looks like some lesion of the spine."

The monkey lay quite still, looking at him with anguished appealing eyes as he continued his manipulation.

"Yes, I thought so," he said. "Fracture of one of the lumbar vertebrae. What luck for me! It's a rare injury, but I've often wondered... and perhaps luck for the monkey too, though that's not very probable. If he was a man and a patient of mine, I shouldn't dare to take the risk. But, as it is..."

Jack Madden started on his southward journey next day, and by the middle of November was at work on his newly discovered cemetery. He and another Englishman were in charge of the excavation, under the control of the Antiquity Department of the Egyptian Government. In order to be close to their work and to avoid the daily ferrying across the Nile from Luxor, they hired a bare roomy native house in the adjoining village of Gurnah. A reef of low sandstone cliffs ran northwards from here towards the temple and terraces of Deir-el-Bahari, and it was in the face of this and on the level below that the ancient graveyard lay. There was much ac-cumulation of sand to be cleared away before the actual exploration of the tombs could begin, but trenches cut below the foot of the sandstone ridge showed that there was an extensive area to investigate.

The more important sepulchres, they found, were hewn in the face of this small cliff: many of these had been rifled in ancient days, for the slabs forming the entrances into them had been split, and some of the mummies unwound, but now and then Madden unearthed some tomb that had escaped these marauders, and in one he found the sarcophagus of a priest of the nineteenth dynasty, and that alone repaid weeks of fruitless work. There were nearly a hundred *ushaptiu* figures of the finest blue glaze; there were four alabaster vessels in which had been placed the viscera of the dead man, removed before embalming; there was a table of which the top was inlaid with squares of variously colored glass, and the legs were of carved ivory and ebony; there were the priest's sandals adorned with exquisite silver filagree; there was his staff of office inlaid with a diaper pattern of cornelian and gold, and on the head of it, forming the handle, was the figure of a squatting cat, carved in amethyst; and the mummy, when unwound, was found to be decked with a necklace of gold plaques and onyx beads. All these were sent down to the Gizeh Museum in Cairo, and Madden reinterred the mummy at the foot of the cliff below the tomb.

He wrote to Hugh Morris describing this find, and laying stress on the unbroken splendor of these crystalline winter days, when from morning to night the sun cruised across the blue, and on the cool nights, when the stars rose and set on the vaporless rim of the desert. If by chance Hugh should change his mind, there was ample room for him in this house at Gurnah, and he would be very welcome.

A fortnight later Madden received a telegram from his friend. It stated that he had been unwell and was starting at once by sea to Port Said, and would come straight up to Luxor. In due course he announced his arrival at Cairo and Madden went across the river next day to meet him; it was reassuring to find him as vital and active as ever, the picture of bronzed health. The two were alone that night, for Madden's colleague had gone for a week's trip up the Nile, and they sat out, when dinner was done, in the enclosed courtyard adjoining the house. Till then Madden had shied off the subject of himself and his health.

"Now I may as well tell you what's been amiss with me," he said, "for I know I look a fearful fraud as an invalid, and physically I've never been better in my life. Every organ has been functioning perfectly except one, but something suddenly went wrong there just once. It was like this."

He paused a moment.

"After you left," he said, "I went on as usual for another month or so, very busy, very serene and, I may say, very successful. Then one morning I arrived at the hospital when there was one perfectly ordinary but major operation waiting for me. The patient, a man, was wheeled into the theater anaesthetized, and I was just about to make the first incision into the abdomen, when I saw that there was sitting on his chest a little gray monkey. It was not looking at me, but at the fold of skin which I held between my thumb and forefinger. I knew, of course, that there was no monkey there, and that what I saw was a hallucination, and I think you'll agree that there was nothing much wrong with my nerves when I tell you that I went through the operation with clear eyes and an unshaking hand. I had to go on; there was no choice about the matter. I couldn't say: "Please take that monkey away, for I knew there was no monkey there." Nor could I say: "Somebody else must do this, as I have a distressing hallucination that there is a monkey sitting on the patient's chest." There would have been an end of me as a surgeon and no mistake. All the time I was at work, it sat there absorbed for the most part in what I was doing and peering into the wound, but now and then it looked up at me, and chattered with rage. Once it fingered a spring-forceps which clipped a severed vein, and that was the worst moment of all...At the end it was carried out still balancing itself on the man's chest...I think I'll have a drink. Strongish, please...Thanks."

"A beastly experience," he said when he had drunk. "Then I went straight away from the hospital to consult my old friend Robert Angus, the alienist and nerve specialist, and told him exactly what had happened to me. He made several tests: he examined my eyes; tried my reflexes; took my blood pressure; there was nothing wrong with any of them. Then he questioned me about my general health and manner of life, and among these questions was one which I am sure has already occurred to you: namely, had anything occurred to me lately, or even remotely, which was likely to make me visualize a monkey? I told him that a few weeks ago a monkey with a broken lumbar vertebrae had crawled on to my lawn, and that I had attempted an operation—binding the broken vertebrae with wire—which had occurred to me before as a possibility. You remember the night, no doubt?"

"Perfectly," said Madden, "I started for Egypt next day. What happened to the monkey, by the way?"

"It lived for two days. I was pleased, because I had expected it would die under the anaesthetic, or immediately afterwards from shock. To get back to what I was telling you. When Angus had asked all his questions, he gave me a good wigging. He said that I had persistently overtaxed my brain for years, without giving it any rest or change of occupation, and that if I wanted to be of any further use in the world, I must drop my work at once for a couple of months. He told me that my brain was tired out and that I had persisted in stimulating it. A man like me, he said, was no better than a confirmed drunkard, and that, as a warning, I had had a touch of an appropriate delirium tremens. The cure was to drop work, just as a drunkard must drop drink. He laid it on hot and strong; he said I was on the verge of a breakdown, entirely owing to my own foolishness, but that I had wonderful physical health, and that if I did break down I should be a disgrace. Above all—and this seemed to me awfully sound advice— he told me not to attempt to avoid thinking about what had happened to me. If I kept my mind off it, I should be perhaps driving it into the subconscious, and then there might be bad trouble. "Rub it in: think what a fool you've been," he said. "Face it, dwell on it, make yourself thoroughly ashamed of yourself." Monkeys, too: I wasn't to avoid the thought of monkeys. In fact, he recommended me to go straight away to the Zoological Gardens, and spend an hour in the monkey-house."

"Odd treatment" interrupted Madden.

"Brilliant treatment. My brain, he explained, had re-belled against its slavery, and had hoisted a red flag with the device of a monkey on it. I must show it that I wasn't fright-ened at its bogus monkeys. I must retort on it by making myself look at dozens of real ones which could bite and maul you savagely, instead of one little sham monkey that had no existence at all. At the same time I must take the red flag seriously, recognize there was danger, and rest. And he prom-ised me that sham monkeys wouldn't trouble me again. Are there any real ones in Egypt, by the way?"

"Not so far as I know," said Madden. "But there must have been once, for there are many images of them in tombs and temples."

"That's good. We'll keep their memory green and my brain cool. Well, there's my story. What do you think of it?"

"Terrifying," said Madden. "But you must have got nerves of iron to get through that operation with the monkey watch-ing."

"A hellish hour. Out of some disordered slime in my brain there had crawled this unbidden thing, which showed itself, apparently substantial, to my eyes. It didn't come from outside; my eyes hadn't told my brain that there was a monkey sitting on the man's chest, but my brain had told my eyes so, making fools of them. I felt as if someone whom I absolutely trusted had played me false. Then again I have wondered whether some instinct in my subconscious mind revolted against vivisection. My reason says that it is justified, for it teaches us how pain can be relieved and death postponed for human beings. But what if my subconscious persuaded my brain to give me a good fright, and reproduce before my eyes the semblance of a monkey, just when I was putting into practice what I had learned from dealing out pain and death to animals?"

He got up suddenly.

"What about bed?" he said. "Five hours sleep was enough for me when I was at work, but now I believe I could sleep the clock around every night."

Young Wilson, Madden's colleague in the excavations, returned the next day and the work went steadily on. One of them was on the spot to start it soon after sunrise, and either one or both of them were superintending it, with an interval of a couple of hours at noon, until sunset. When the mere work of clearing the face of the sandstone cliff and of carting away the silted soil was in progress, the presence of one of them sufficed. For there was nothing to do but to see that the workmen shoveled industriously, and passed regularly with their baskets of earth and sand on their shoulders to the dumping grounds, which stretched away from the area to be excavated, in lengthening peninsulas of trodden soil. But, as they advanced along the sandstone ridge, there would now and then appear a chiselled smoothness in the cliff and then both must be alert. There was great excitement to see if, when they exposed the hewn slab that formed the door into the tomb, it had escaped ancient marauders, and still stood in place and intact for the modern to explore. But now, for many days they came upon no sepulchre that had not already been opened. The mummy, in these cases, had been unwound in the search for necklaces and scarabs, and its scattered bones lay about. Madden was always at pains to reinter these.

At first Hugh Morris was assiduous in watching the excavations, but as day after day went by without anything of interest turning up, his attendance grew less frequent; it was too much of a holiday to watch the day-long removal of sand from one place to another. He visited the Tomb of the Kings, and went across the river and saw the temples at Karnak, but his appetite for antiquities was small. On other days he rode in the desert, or spent the day with friends at one of the Luxor hotels. He came home from there one evening in rare good spirits, for he had played lawn-tennis with a woman on whom he had operated for a malignant tumor six months before, and she had skipped about the court like a two-year-old. "God, how I want to be at work again," he exclaimed. "I wonder whether I ought not to have stuck it out, and defied my brain to frighten me with bogies."

The weeks passed on, and now there were but two days left before his return to England, where he hoped to resume work at once; his tickets were taken and his berth booked. As he sat over breakfast that morning with Wilson, there came a workman from the excavation, with a note scribbled in hot haste to Madden, to say that they had just come upon a tomb which seemed to be unrifled, for the slab that closed it was in place and unbroken. To Wilson, the news was like the sight of a sail to a marooned mariner, and when, a quarter of an hour later, Morris followed him, he was just in time to see the slab pried away. There was no sarcophagus within, for the rock wall did duty for that, but there lay there, varnished and bright in hue as if painted yesterday, the mummy-case roughly following the outline of the human form. By it stood the alabaster vases containing the entrails of the dead, and at each corner of the sepulchre, there were carved out of the sandstone rock, forming, as it were, pillars to support the roof, thick-set images of squatting apes. The mummy-case was hoisted out and carried away by workmen on a bier of boards into the courtyard of the excavator's house at Gurnah, for the opening of it and the unwrapping of the dead.

They got to work that evening directly after they had fed. The face painted on the lid was that of a girl or young woman, and presently deciphering the hieroglyphic inscription, Madden read out that within lay the body of A-pen-ara, daughter of the overseer of the cattle of Senmut.

"Then follow the usual formulas," he said. "Yes, yes...ah, you'll be interested in this, Hugh, for you asked me once about it. A-pen-ara curses any who desecrates or meddles with her bones, and should anyone do so, the guardians of her sepulchre will see to him, and he shall die childless and in panic and agony; also the guardians of her sepulchre will tear the hair from his head and scoop his eyes from their sockets, and pluck the thumb from his right hand, as a man plucks the young blade of corn from its sheath."

Morris laughed.

"Very pretty little attentions," he said. "And who are the guardians of this sweet young lady's sepulchre? Those four great apes carved at the corners?"

"No doubt. But we won't trouble them, for tomorrow I shall bury Miss A-pen-ara's bones again with all decency in the trench at the foot of her tomb. They'll be safer there, for if we put them back where we found them, there would be pieces of her hawked about by half the donkey-boys in Luxor in a few days. 'Buy a mummy hand, lady?... Foot of a Gypsy Queen, only ten piastres, gentlemen'... Now for the unwinding."

It was dark by now, and Wilson fetched out a paraffin lamp, which burned unwaveringly in the still air. The lid of the mummy-case was easily detached, and within was the slim swaddled body. The embalming had not been very thoroughly done, for all the skin and flesh had perished from the head, leaving only bones of the skull stained brown with bitumen. Round it was a mop of hair, which with the ingress of the air subsided like a belated souffle, and crumbled into dust. The cloth that swathed the body was as brittle, but around the neck, still just holding together, was a collar of curious and rare workmanship: little ivory figures of squatting apes alternated with silver beads. But again a touch broke the thread that strung them together, and each had to be picked out singly. A bracelet of scarabs and cornelians still clasped one of the fleshless wrists. They turned the body over in order to get at the member of the necklace which lay beneath the nape. The rotted mummy-cloth fell away altogether from the back, disclosing the shoulder-blades and the spine down as far as the pelvis. Here the embalming had been better done, for the bones still held together with remnants of muscle and cartilage.

Hugh Morris suddenly sprang to his feet.

"My God, look there!" he cried, "one of the lumbar vertebrae, there at the base of the spine, has been broken and clamped together with a metal band. To hell with your antiquities; let me come and examine something much more modern than any of us!"

He pushed Jack Madden aside, and peered at this marvel of surgery. "Put the lamp closer," he said, as if directing some nurse at an operation. "Yes, that vertebra had been broken right across and has been clamped together. No one has ever, as far as I know, attempted such an operation except myself, and I have only performed it on that little paralyzed monkey that crept into my garden one night. But some Egyptian surgeon, more than three thousand years ago, performed it on a woman. And look, look! She lived afterwards, for the broken vertebra put out that bony efflorescence of healing which has encroached over the metal band. That's a slow process, and it must have taken place during her lifetime, for there is no such energy in a corpse. The woman lived long; probably she recovered completely. And my wretched little monkey only lived two days and was dying all the time."

Those questing hawk-visioned fingers of the surgeon perceived more finely than actual sight, and now he closed his eyes as the tip of them felt their way about the fracture in the broken vertebra and the clamping metal band.

"The band doesn't encircle the bone," he said, "and there are no studs attaching it. There must have been a spring in it, which, when it was clasped there, keep it tight. It has been clamped around the bone itself; the surgeon must have scraped the vertebra clean of flesh before he attached it. I would give two years of my life to have looked on, like a student, at that masterpiece of skill, and it was worthwhile giving up two months of my work only to have seen the result.

And the injury itself is so rare, this breaking of a spinal vertebra. To be sure, the hangman does something of the sort, but there's no mending that! Good Lord, my holiday has not been a waste of time!"

Madden settled that it was not worthwhile to send the mummy-case to the museum at Gizeh, for it was of a very ordinary type, and when the examination was over they lifted the body back into it, for reinterment next day. It was now long after midnight and presently the house was dark.

Hugh Morrison slept on the ground floor in a room adjoining the yard where the mummy-case lay. He remained long awake marvelling at that astonishing piece of surgical skill performed, according to Madden, some thirty-five centuries ago. So occupied had his mind been with homage that not till now did he realize that the tangible proof and witness of the operation would tomorrow be buried again and lost to science. He must persuade Madden to let him detach at least three of the vertebrae, the mended one and those immediately above and below it, and take them back to England as demonstration of what could be done; he would lecture on his exhibit and present it to the Royal College of Surgeons for example and incitement. Other trained eyes beside his own must see what had been successfully achieved by some unknown operator in the nineteenth dynasty... But supposing Madden refused? He always made a point of scrupulously reburying these remains; it was a principle with him, and no doubt some superstition complex—the hardest of all to combat because of its sheer unreasonableness—was involved. Briefly, it was impossible to risk the chance of his refusal.

He got out of bed, listened for a moment by his door, and then softly went out into the yard. The moon had risen, for the brightness of the stars had paled, and though no direct rays shone into the walled enclosure, the dusk was dispersed by the toneless luminosity of the sky, and he had no need of a lamp. He drew the lid off the coffin, and folded back the tattered cerements which Madden had replaced over the body.

He had thought that those lower vertebrae of which he was determined to possess himself would be easily detached, so far perished were the muscle and cartilage which held them together; but they cohered as if they had been clamped, and it required the utmost force of his powerful fingers to snap the spine, and as he did so the severed bones cracked as with the noise of a pistol-shot. But there was no sign that anyone in the house had heard it; there came no sound of steps, nor lights in the windows. One more fracture was needed, and then the relic was his. Before he replaced the ragged clothes he looked again at the stained fleshless bones. Shadow dwelt in the empty eye-sockets, as if black sunken eyes still lay there, fixed, regarding him; the lipless mouth snarled and grimaced. Even as he looked some change came over its aspect, and for one brief moment he fancied that there lay staring up at him the face of a great brown ape. But instantly that illusion vanished, and replacing the lid he went back to his room.

The mummy-case was reinterred next day, and two evenings after, Morris left Luxor by the night train for Cairo, to join a homeward-bound P & O at Port Said. There were some hours to spare before his ship sailed, and having deposited his luggage, including a locked leather dispatch-case, on board, he lunched at the Café Tewfik near the quay. There was a garden in front of it with palm trees and trellises gaily clad in bougainvillias; a low wooden rail separated it from the street, and Morris had a table close to this. As he ate he watched the polychromatic pageant of Eastern life passing by; there were Egyptian officials in broadcloth frock coats and red fezzes; barefooted splay-toed fellahin in blue gabardines; veiled women in white making stealthy eyes at passers-by; half-naked guttersnipe, one with a sprig of scarlet hibiscus behind his ear; travellers from India with solar topees and an air of aloof British superiority; dishevelled sons of the Prophet in green turbans; a stately sheik in a white burnous; French painted ladies of a professional class with lace-rimmed parasols and provocative glances; a wild-eyed dervish in an accordion-pleated skirt, chewing betel-nut and slightly foaming at the mouth. A Greek boot-black with a box adorned with brass plaques tapped his brushes on it to encourage customers; an Egyptian girl squatted in the gutter beside a gramophone; steamers passing into the Canal hooted on their sirens.

Then at the edge of the pavement there sauntered by a young Italian harnessed to a barrel-organ; with one hand he ground out a popular air by Verdi, in the other he held out a tin can for the tributes of music lovers; a small monkey in a yellow jacket, tethered to his wrist, sat on the top of his instrument. The musician had come opposite the table where Morris sat; Morris liked the gay tinkling tune, and feeling in his pocket for a piastre, he beckoned to him. The boy grinned and stepped up to the rail.

Then suddenly the melancholy-eyed monkey leaped from its place on the organ and sprang onto the table by which Morris sat. It alighted there, chattering with rage in a crash of broken glass. A flower vase was upset, a plate clattered onto the floor. Morris's coffee cup discharged its black contents on the tablecloth. Next moment the Italian had twitched the frenzied little beast back to him, and it fell head downwards on the pavement. A shrill hubbub arose; the waiter at Morris's table hurried up with voluble execrations; a policeman kicked at the monkey as it lay on the ground; the barrel-organ tottered and crashed on the roadway. Then all subsided again, and the Italian boy picked up the little body from the pavement. He held it out in his hand to Morris.

"E morto." he said.

"Serve it right, too," retorted Morris. "Why did it fly at me like that?"

He traveled back to London by long sea, and day after day that tragic little incident, in which he had had no responsible part, began to make a sort of coloring matter in his mind during those hours of lazy leisure on shipboard, when a man gives about an equal inattention to the book he reads and to what passes around him. Sometimes if the shadow of a seagull overhead slid across the deck towards him, there leaped into his brain, before his eyes could reassure him, the ludicrous fancy that this shadow was a monkey springing at him. One day they ran into a gale from the west; there was a crash of glass at his elbow as a sudden lurch of the ship upset a laden steward, and Morris jumped from his seat thinking that a monkey had leaped onto his table again. There was a cinematograph show in the salon one evening, in which some naturalist exhibited the films he had taken of wildlife in Indian jungles; when he put on the screen the picture of a company of monkeys swinging their way through the trees, Morris involuntarily clutched the sides of his chair in hideous panic that lasted but a fraction of a second, until he recalled to himself that he was only looking at a film in the salon of a steamer passing up the coast of Portugal. He came sleepy into his cabin one night and saw some animal crouching by the locked leather dispatch-case. His breath caught in his throat before he perceived that this was a friendly cat which rose with gleaming eyes and arched its back. . . .

These fantastic unreasonable alarms were disquieting. He had as yet no repetition of the hallucination that he saw a monkey, but some deep-buried "idea," to cure which he had taken two months' holiday, was still unpurged from his mind. He must consult Robert Angus again when he got home, and seek further advice. Probably that incident at Port Said had rekindled the obscure trouble, and there was this added to it, that he knew he was now frightened of real monkeys; there was terror sprouting in the dark of his soul. But as for it having any connection with his pilfered treasure, so rank and childish a superstition deserved only the ridicule he gave it. Often he unlocked his leather case and sat pouring over that miracle of surgery which made practical again long-forgotten dexterities.

But it was good to be back in England. For the last three days of the voyage no menace had flashed out on him from the unknown dusks, and surely he had been disquieting himself in vain. There was a light mist lying over Regent's Park on this warm March evening, and a drizzle of rain was falling. He made an appointment for the next morning with the specialist. He telephoned to the hospital that he had returned, and hoped to resume work at once. He dined in very good spirits, talking to his manservant, and, as subsequently came out, he showed him his treasured bones, telling him that he had taken the relic from a mummy which he had seen unwrapped, and that he meant to lecture on it. When he went up to bed he carried the leather case with him. Bed was comfortable after the ship's berth, and through his open window came the soft hissing of the rain onto the shrubs outside.

His servant slept in the room immediately over his. A little before dawn he woke with a start, roused by horrible cries from somewhere close at hand. Then came the words yelled out in a voice that he knew:

"Help! Help!" it cried. "O my God, my God! Ah-h———" and it rose to a scream again.

The man hurried down and clicked on the light in his master's room as he entered. The cries had ceased; only a low moaning came from the bed. A huge ape with busy hands was bending over it; then, taking up the body that lay there, by the neck and the hips, he bent it backwards and it cracked like a dry stick. Then it tore open the leather case that was on a table by the bedside, and with something that gleamed white in its dripping fingers, it shambled to the window and disappeared.

A doctor arrived within half an hour, but too late. Handfuls of hair with flaps of skin attached had been torn from the head of the murdered man, both eyes were scooped out of their sockets, the right thumb had been plucked off the hand, and the back was broken across the lower vertebrae.

Nothing has since come to light which could rationally explain the tragedy. No large ape had escaped from the neighboring Zoological Garden, or, as far as could be ascertained, from elsewhere, nor was the monstrous visitor of that night ever seen again. Morris's servant had only had the briefest sight of it, and his description of it at the inquest did not tally with that of any known simian type. And the sequel was even more mysterious, for Madden, returning to England at the close of the season in Egypt, had asked Morris's servant exactly what it was that his master had shown him the evening before as having been taken by him from a mummy which he had seen unwrapped, and had got from him a sufficiently conclusive account of it. Next autumn he continued his excavations in the cemetery of Gurnah, and he disinterred once more the mummy-case of A-pen-ara and opened it. But the spinal vertebrae were all in place and complete; one had around it the silver clip which Morris had hailed as a unique achievement in surgery.

THE WOLVES OF CERNOGRATZ

Saki

"Are there any old legends attached to the castle?" asked Conrad of his sister. Conrad was a prosperous Hamburg merchant, but he was the one poetically-dispositioned member of an eminently practical family.

The Baroness Gruebel shrugged her plump shoulders.

"There are always legends hanging about these old places. They are not difficult to invent and they cost nothing. In this case there is a story that when anyone dies in the castle all the dogs in the village and the wild beasts in the forest howl the night long. It would not be pleasant to listen to, would it?"

"It would be weird and romantic," said the Hamburg merchant.

"Anyhow, it isn't true," said the Baroness complacently. "Since we bought the place we have had proof that nothing of the sort happens. When the old mother-in-law died last springtime we all listened, but there was no howling. It is just a story that lends dignity to the place without costing anything."

"The story is not as you have told it," said Amalie, the

gray old governess. Everyone turned and looked at her in astonishment. She was wont to sit silent and prim and faded in her place at the table, never speaking unless someone spoke to her, and there were few who troubled themselves to make conversation with her. Today a sudden volubility had descended on her; she continued to talk, rapidly and nervously, looking straight in front of her and seeming to address no one in particular.

"It is not when *anyone* dies in the castle that the howling is heard. It was when one of the Cernogratz family died at the edge of the forest just before the death hour. There were only a few wolves that had their lairs in this part of the forest, but at such a time the keepers say there would be scores of them, gliding about in the shadows and howling in chorus, and the dogs of the castle and the village and all the farms around would bay and howl in fear and anger at the wolf chorus, and as the soul of the dying one left its body a tree would crash down in the park. That is what happened when a Cernogratz died in his family castle. But for a stranger dying here, of course no wolf would howl and no tree would fall. Oh, no."

There was a note of defiance, almost of contempt, in her voice as she said the last words. The well-fed, much too well-dressed Baroness stared angrily at the dowdy old woman who had come forth from her usual and seemly position of effacement to speak so disrespectfully.

"You seem to know quite a lot about the von Cernogratz legends, Fräulein Schmidt," she said sharply. "I did not know that family histories were among the subjects you are supposed to be proficient in."

The answer to her taunt was even more unexpected and astonishing than the conversational outbreak which had provoked it.

"I am a von Cernogratz myself," said the old woman. "That is why I know the family history."

"You a von Cernogratz? You!" came in an incredulous chorus.

"When we became very poor," she explained, "and I had to go out and give teaching lessons, I took another name; I thought it would be more in keeping. But my grandfather spent much of his time as a·boy in this castle, and my father used to tell me many stories about it, and of course, I knew all the family legends and stories. When one has nothing left to oneself but memories, one guards and dusts them with special care. I little thought, when I took service with you, that I should one day come with you to the old home of my family. I could wish it had been anywhere else."

There was silence when she finished speaking, and then the Baroness turned the conversation to a less embarrassing topic than family histories. But afterwards, when the old governess had slipped away quietly to her duties, there arose a clamor of derision and disbelief.

"It was an impertinence," snapped the Baron, his protruding eyes taking on a scandalized expression. "Fancy the woman talking like that at our table! She almost told us we were nobodies, and I don't believe a word of it. She is just Schmidt and nothing more. She has been talking to some of the peasants about the old Cernogratz family, and raked up their history and their stories."

"She wants to make herself out as of some consequence," said the Baroness. "She knows she will soon be past work and she wants to appeal to our sympathies. Her grandfather, indeed!"

The Baroness had the usual number of grandfathers, but she never boasted about them.

"I dare say her grandfather was a pantry boy or something of the sort in the castle," sniggered the Baron. "That part of the story may be true."

The merchant from Hamburg said nothing; he had seen tears in the old woman's eyes when she spoke of guarding her memories—or, being of an imaginative disposition, he thought he had.

"I shall give her notice to go as soon as the New Year festivities are over," said the Baroness. "Till then I shall be too busy to manage without her."

But she had to manage without her all the same, for in the cold biting weather after Christmas, the old governess fell ill and kept to her room.

"It is most provoking," said the Baroness, as her guests sat around the fire on one of the last evenings of the dying year. "All the time that she has been with us I cannot remember that she was ever seriously ill, too ill to go about and do her work, I mean. And now, when I have the house full, and she could be useful in so many ways, she goes and breaks down. One is sorry for her, of course, she looks so withered and shrunken, but it is intensely annoying all the same."

"Most annoying," agreed the banker's wife sympathetically. "It is the intense cold, I expect, it breaks the old people up. It has been unusually cold this year."

"The frost is the sharpest that has been known in December for many years," said the Baron.

"And, of course, she *is* quite old," said the Baroness. "I wish I had given her notice some weeks ago, then she would have left before this happened to her. Why, Wappi, what is the matter with you?"

The small, woolly lap dog had leapt suddenly down from its cushion and crept, shivering, under the sofa. At the same moment an outburst of angry barking came from the dogs in the castle yard, and other dogs could be heard yapping and barking in the distance.

"What is disturbing the animals?" asked the Baron.

And then the humans, listening intently, heard the sound that had roused the dogs to their demonstrations of fear and rage; heard a long-drawn whining howl, rising and falling, seeming at one moment leagues away, at others sweeping across the snow until it appeared to come from the foot of the castle walls. All the starved, cold misery of a frozen world, all the relentless hungry-fury of the wild, blended with other forlorn and haunting melodies to which one could give no name, seemed concentrated in that wailing cry.

"Wolves!" cried the Baron.

Their music broke forth in one raging burst, seeming to come from everywhere.

"Hundreds of wolves," said the Hamburg merchant, who was a man of strong imagination.

Moved by some impulse which she could not have explained, the Baroness left her guests and made her way to the narrow, cheerless room where the old governess lay watching the hours of the dying year slip by. In spite of the biting cold of the winter night, the window stood open. With a scandalized exclamation on her lips, the Baroness rushed forward to close it.

"Leave it open," said the old woman in a voice that for all its weakness carried an air of command such as the Baroness had never heard before from her lips.

"But you will die of cold!" she expostulated.

"I am dying in any case," said the voice, "and I want to hear their music. They have come from far and wide to sing the death-music of my family. It is beautiful that they have come; I am the last von Cernogratz that will die in our old castle, and they have come to sing to me. Hark, how loud they are calling!"

The cry of the wolves rose on the still winter air and floated around the castle walls in long-drawn piercing wails. The old woman lay back on her couch with a look of long-delayed happiness on her face.

"Go away," she said to the Baroness. "I am not lonely any more. I am one of a great old family...."

"I think she is dying," said the Baroness when she had

rejoined her guests. "I suppose we must send for a doctor. And that terrible howling! Not for much money would I have such death-music."

"That music is not to be bought for any amount of money," said Conrad.

"Hark! What is that other sound?" asked the Baron, as a noise of splitting and crashing was heard.

It was a tree falling in the park.

There was a moment of constrained silence, and then the banker's wife spoke.

"It is the intense cold that is splitting the trees. It is also the cold that has brought the wolves out in such numbers. It is many years since we have had such a cold winter."

The Baroness eagerly agreed that the cold was responsible for these things. It was the cold of the open window, too, which caused the heart failure that made the doctor's ministrations unnecessary for the old Fräulein. But the death notice in the newspapers looked very well:

"On December 29th, at Schloss Cernogratz, Amalie von Cernogratz, for many years the valued friend of Baron and Baroness Gruebel passed away."

THE MONSTER OF POOT HOLLER

Ida Chittum

Poot Holler is a dangerous place.

The grasshoppers there are big and mean. They chew tobacco and spit the juice in folk's eyes and hop off hootin'. They can't be found or tracked down for blendin' with the scenery.

The Holler is so full of snakes and crawling creepy things, they wear smooth paths in the grass coming and going.

To say nothing of the beasts and birds of two and four legs, that lay in wait both behind bush and in treetop, waiting the unwary with sharp claws, beak and eager eye.

Folk in other parts of the mountains look down on Poot Hollerians. They say the laziest men and the biggest liars live there too, and men folk who would rather tell a lie on credit than to tell the truth for cash. The land there is so poor, rabbits have to carry greens to cross it. That's how we came to be in Poot Holler. Sledge Kunkle's Pa's a patch farmer there.

All the Kunkles are born warriors and adventurers. Duck Kunkle, a cousin of Sledge, came down off Mount Baldy a-calling on Sledge. He came to get a good look at the monster of Poot Holler.

The evening was damp with rags of fog a-flying in the wind.

"Just the kind of night the monster likes to crawl out and look around," Sledge said.

He was speaking to Duck in their private place behind the wood pile.

"I'll go down into the holler alone. You stay up on the hill. Then the monster can't lay hold of both of us at the same time."

Sledge picked up a hefty stick of green wood. He passed it to Duck.

"Carry this club. Keep it handy."

So they started out to hunt the monster of Poot Holler. They followed the ghost of a path into the trees. The woods became darker and denser. The only open place for miles around was the dreaded Dunn's Meadow. The place of the ravine. The home of the monster of Poot Holler.

Dunn himself had vanished long ago. Disappeared. Vanished on just such a night as this. A damp and foggy evening.

The tale had been told over and over to eager, fearful listeners.

On nearing Dunn's Meadow, the boys spoke only in whispers and then were altogether silent.

Standing side-by-side, they gazed slitty-eyed down into the holler. A clean, green patch of grass, so innocent in itself but cut through down the middle with a nasty gash. The ravine. The home of the monster of Poot Holler. The steep banks reared up jagged and red-rimmed as a fresh-cut throat.

Sledge caught his breath. The old folks were right. Something strangely other-worldish and death-dealing could live in those slimy muddy depths. It could slip out on misty nights and prowl.

"There are those that take joy in scoffing at what they know little about," Aunt Hazy told Sledge when he doubted.

Just now gazing down into the brackish water, Sledge

and Duck moved closer together. They imagined the brave little Jesus bugs walking on the dangerous surface.

"You really think a monster lives down there?" Duck asked, now not so brave as he had been back at the wood pile.

His head was full of scary thoughts. He stood stiff and straight. His hands shoved down in his pockets.

"You think we should go back home?"

Duck reached out and laid a hand on his cousin's shoulder.

Sledge jumped. He feared for one foolish second the monster of Poot Holler had already come to claim him. He shook his head. A Kunkle couldn't retreat. No way. Never had. Never would.

"You stay here," Sledge said. "Keep that club handy just in case. I'm going down into the meadow. If there is something in that mud..." He turned to face Duck nose on.

"I want to see what it is."

Duck watched his cousin Sledge go down the hill in the gathering twilight. A chill crept up his spine. He buttoned his shirt at the throat. He inched down bracing his back against the tree. He propped the green club at his side and waited.

"There were," Aunt Hazy had said, "more strange things in heaven and on earth than were sang of in song or story."

If so, Duck reckoned, he did not want to meet up with them. At the same time he longed to know what they might look like.

Was one of them the monster of Poot Holler?

He got to his feet watching in the gloom, listening, thinking.

Sledge was a fast runner. That could save him from the monster. Sledge went so fast he could pass up a tracking dog and tree the 'coon himself. He was a boy who depended upon his skills and speed. But—*that* monster in the ravine in dreaded Dunn's Meadow, might be a different matter.

Duck stood in the swirling mist recalling.

"Wouldn't care to go there myself," Sledge's Pa had said. "'Tis fearsome. A place only to be looked at from a distance. And that on bright and sunny days. A cursed and perilous pit." Pa broke off as he took a hearty chew of plug. He spit and caught a fly on the wing.

"You'll never see a sensible cow or mule grazing there. An instinct for danger warns them away. Animals sense in their own natural way the hidden menace of that ravine."

(A tale told, the boys had decided, to keep them in nights, and them going onto fourteen years of age.)

Now out in the dark alone, Duck was not so sure. Now that he was on that very spot.

"The last dead man was found there and that not so long ago. Cold and dead-looking as if he had been put through a bale binder."

Pa's tale went on.

"Handson Nash found him. Seen what he took for a man lying asleep, he crept down the hill. Never should have went. The man lay face down, all flung out crooked and cattywampus. His face the pale of fish belly and all twisted with pain. 'Twas enough to make a grown man race off. Thet's what he did. Run off and came here. The body looked as if wire had been wound 'round it every few inches."

Duck shook his head to quit thinking of the old tale.

He shivered. Could something like that happen to Sledge?

"There were no tracks," Pa had said. "Just a rippling in the clay that didn't belong there. A man born and raised in Poot Holler could tell."

Duck wiped cold sweat from his brow.

Sledge was down there alone. But—Sledge was armed. His pockets were full of stones. And he had a true arm for throwing straight as a gun shoots. So true that a squirrel near his place didn't dar'st come closer'n fifty foot of the ground.

But—would all that do him any good against the monster

of Poot Holler? Night had come. The trees all around had lost their bright colors and become bleak as Duck's thoughts.

Then he heard a cry. His blood turned to ice.

One piercing anguished cry in Sledge's voice. That one long drawn-out cry. Nothing more.

With no thought but to save Sledge, Duck went slamming down the hill, the green club forgotten.

The monster of Poot Holler had come out of the ravine. It lay draped over the edge. Thin as bailing wire. Long as a full-grown tree. The monster hung there lashing and threshing and holding onto Sledge. The monster had already twisted around Sledge. So he appeared to be bound with shining wet steel wire, wrapped like a package. A limp, cold motionless bundle. The monster was a living hungry wire. On one end Duck could see the wet red snapping mouth, darting in at Sledge ready to draw the lifeblood. To suck him dry. On sensing Duck, the wet red mouth opened wider. The head swiveled in his direction. As Duck worked in closer, the thready head swayed, rose and fell. A thing without eyes seeking him out by warmth and scent.

In frantic haste Duck grabbed up and used the only weapon at hand. Dry grass and a match from his pocket. He caught up handfuls of dry grass, setting it ablaze. Racing in at the lashing monster holding Sledge prisoner, he crushed the flaming grass torch again and again upon that awful twisting length. Burning his own hands, searing his arms, choking on the acid smoke, yet not feeling the pain, he fought. Struggling on in violent, silent battle, with wild leaps, with blazing flame, in the rising light of the full moon, Duck fought a raging battle with the monster of Poot Holler. Dodging, turning away, racing back, as the whipping, living string-thing tried to hold onto Sledge and catch him too. Catch them both, wrap them like sausages and drag them down to eat, slowly in the depths of the ooze.

Duck laid hold on Sledge as tender as he could with his

own sore hands. He dragged him over the burned, scorched ground and sharp stones. For he wanted with all his heart to get away from Dunn's Meadow. Before the monster cooled off and came back for them.

The cousins stumbled blindly through the night up hill and down, Duck supporting Sledge, resting and then moving on again. By dawn their clothing was ripped to rags. They were weak and bleeding and cold and hungry. Duck, his hands still shaking, caught fish and they cooked them in leaves over a fire. They washed themselves and their clothing as best they could. They stayed out of the way of folks until Sledge could make other sounds besides gibberish.

Pa knew at the sight of them, something awful had happened.

"But," he said "those that don't heed their elders have to learn the hard way." Their story came out piece by piece, how they had seen and fought with the monster of Poot Holler.

Sledge and Duck never again, in their whole lives long, returned to the ravine in the dreaded Dunn's Meadow, where, neither doubts, still lives deep in the blackish-green muck, a living strangling steel-like wire.

The monster of Poot Holler.

A MOST UNUSUAL MURDER

Robert Bloch

"Only the dead know Brooklyn."

Thomas Wolfe said that, and he's dead now, so he ought to know.

London, of course, is a different story.

At least that's the way Hilary Kane thought of it. Not as a story, perhaps, but rather as an old-fashioned, outsize picaresque novel in which every street was a chapter crammed with characters and incidents of its own. Each block a page, each structure a separate paragraph unto itself within the sprawling, tangled plot—such was Hilary Kane's concept of the city, and he knew it well.

Over the years he strolled the pavements, reading the city, sentence by sentence, until every line was familiar; he'd learned London by heart.

And that's why he was so startled when, one bleak afternoon late in November, he discovered the shop in Saxe-Coburg Square.

"I'll be damned!" he said.

"Probably." Lester Woods, his companion, took the edge

off the affirmation with an indulgent smile. "What's the problem?"

"This." Kane gestured toward the tiny window of the establishment nestled inconspicuously between two residential relics of Victoria's day.

"An antique place." Woods nodded. "At the rate they're springing up, there must be at least one for every tourist in London."

"But not here." Kane frowned. "I happen to have come by this way less than a week ago, and I'd swear there was no shop in the Square."

"Then it must have opened since." The two men moved up to the entrance, glancing through the display window in passing.

Kane's frown deepened. "You call this new? Look at the dust on those goblets."

"Playing detective again, eh?" Woods shook his head. "Trouble with you, Hilary, is that you have too many hobbies." He glanced across the Square as a chill wind heralded the coming of twilight. "Getting late—we'd better move along."

"Not until I find out about this."

Kane was already opening the door and Woods sighed. "The game is afoot, I suppose. All right, let's get it over with."

The shop-bell tinkled and the two men stepped inside. The door closed, the tinkling stopped, and they stood in the shadows and the silence.

But one of the shadows was not silent. It rose from behind the single counter in the small space before the rear wall.

"Good afternoon, gentlemen," said the shadow, and switched on an overhead light. It cast a dim nimbus over the countertop and gave dimension to the shadow, revealing the substance of a diminutive figure with an unremarkable face beneath a balding brow.

Kane addressed the proprietor. "Mind if we have a look?"

"Is there any special area of interest?" The proprietor

gestured toward the shelves lining the wall behind him. "Books, maps, china, crystal?"

"Not really," Kane said. "It's just that I'm always curious about a new shop of this sort————"

The proprietor shook his head. "Begging your pardon, but it's hardly new."

Woods glanced at his friend with a barely suppressed smile, but Kane ignored him.

"Odd," Kane said. "I've never noticed this place before."

"Quite so. I've been in business a good many years, but this is a new location."

Now it was Kane's turn to glance quickly at Woods, and his smile was not suppressed. But Woods was already eyeing the artifacts on display, and after a moment Kane began his own inspection.

Peering at the shelving beneath the glass counter, he made a rapid inventory. He noted a boudoir lamp with a beaded fringe, a "lavaliere," a tray of pearly buttons, a durbar souvenir program, and a framed and inscribed photograph of Matilda Alice Victoria Wood alias Bella Delmare alias Marie Lloyd. There was a miscellany of old jewelry, hunting watches, pewter mugs, napkin rings, a toy bank in the shape of a miniature Crystal Palace, and a display poster of a formidably mustached Lord Kitchener with his gloved finger extended in a gesture of imperious command.

It was, he decided, the mixture as before. Nothing unusual, and most of it—like the Kitchener poster—not even properly antique but merely outmoded. Those fans on the bottom shelf, for example, and the silk toppers, the opera glasses, the black bag in the far corner covered with what was once called "American cloth."

Something about the phrase caused Kane to stoop and make a closer inspection. American cloth. Dusty now, but once shiny, like the tarnished silver nameplate identifying its owner. He read the inscription:

J. Ridley, M.D.

Kane looked up, striving to conceal his sudden surge of excitement.

Impossible! It couldn't be—and yet it was. Keeping his voice and gesture carefully casual, he indicated the bag to the proprietor.

"A medical kit?"

"Yes, I imagine so."

"Might I ask where you acquired it?"

The little man shrugged. "Hard to remember. In this line one picks up the odd item here and there over the years."

"Might I have a look at it, please?"

The elderly proprietor lifted the bag to the countertop. Woods stared at it, puzzled, but Kane ignored him, his gaze intent on the nameplate below the lock. "Would you mind opening it?" he said.

"I'm afraid I don't have the key."

Kane reached out and pressed the lock; it was rusted, but firmly fixed. Frowning, he lifted the bag and shook it gently.

Something jiggled inside, and as he heard the click of metal against metal his elation peaked. Somehow he suppressed it as he spoke.

"How much are you asking?"

The proprietor was equally emotionless. "Not for sale."

"But—"

"Sorry, sir. It's against my policy to dispose of blind items. And since there's no telling what's inside————"

"Look, it's only an old medical bag. I hardly imagine it contains the Crown jewels."

In the background Woods snickered, but the proprietor ignored him. "Granted," he said. "But one can't be certain of the contents." Now the little man lifted the bag and once again there was a clicking sound. "Coins, perhaps."

"Probably just surgical instruments," Kane said impatiently. "Why don't you force the lock and settle the matter?"

"Oh, I couldn't do that. It would destroy its value."

"What value?" Kane's guard was down now; he knew he'd made a tactical error but he couldn't help himself.

The proprietor smiled, "I told you the bag is not for sale."

"Everything has its price."

Kane's statement was a challenge, and the proprietor's smile broadened as he met it. "One hundred pounds."

"A hundred pounds for *that?*" Woods grinned—then gaped at Kane's response.

"Done and done."

"But, sir————"

For answer Kane drew out his wallet and extracted five twenty-pound notes. Placing them on the countertop, he lifted the bag and moved toward the door. Woods followed hastily, turning to close the door behind him.

The proprietor gestured. "Wait—come back————"

But Kane was already hurrying down the street, clutching the black bag under his arm.

He was still clutching it half an hour later as Woods moved with him into the spacious study of Kane's flat overlooking the verdant vista of Cadogan Square. Dappled splotches of sunlight reflected from the gleaming oilcloth as Kane set the bag on the table and carefully wiped away the film of dust with a dampened rag. He smiled triumphantly at Woods.

"Looks a bit better now, don't you think?"

"I don't think anything." Woods shook his head. "A hundred pounds for an old medical kit————"

"A *very* old medical kit," said Kane. "Dates back to the Eighties, if I'm not mistaken."

"Even so, I hardly see————"

"Of course you wouldn't! I doubt if anyone besides myself would attach much significance to the name of J. Ridley, M.D."

"Never heard of him."

"That's understandable." Kane smiled. "He preferred to call himself Jack the Ripper."

"Jack the Ripper?"

"Surely you know the case. Whitechapel, 1888—the savage slaying and mutilation of prostitutes by a cunning mass murderer who taunted the police—a shadow, stalking his prey in the streets."

Woods frowned. "But he was never caught, was he? Not even identified."

"In that you're mistaken. No murderer has been identified quite as frequently as Red Jack. At the time of the crimes and over the years since, a score of suspects were named. A prime candidate was the Pole, Klosowski, alias George Chapman, who killed several wives—but poison was his method and gain his motive, whereas the Ripper's victims were all penniless prostitutes who died under the knife. Another convicted murderer, Neil Cream, even openly proclaimed *he* was the Ripper———"

"Wouldn't that be the answer, then?"

Kane shrugged. "Unfortunately, Cream happened to be in America at the time of the Ripper murders. Egomania prompted his false confession." He shook his head. "Then there was John Pizer, a bookbinder known by the nickname of 'Leather Apron'—he was actually arrested, but quickly cleared and released. Some think the killings were the work of a Russian called Konovalov who also went by the name of Pedachenko and worked as a barber's surgeon; supposedly he was a Tsarist secret agent who perpetrated the slayings to discredit the British police."

"Sounds pretty far-fetched if you ask me."

"Exactly." Kane smiled. "But there are other candidates, equally improbable. Montague John Druitt for one, a barrister of unsound mind who drowned himself in the Thames shortly after the last Ripper murder. Unfortunately, it has been established that he was living in Bournemouth, and on the days before and after the final slaying he was there, playing cricket. Then there was the Duke of Clarence———"

"Who?"

"Queen Victoria's grandson in direct line of succession to the throne."

"Surely you're not serious?"

"No, but others are. It has been asserted that Clarence was a known deviate who suffered from insanity as the result of venereal infection, and that his death in 1892 was actually due to the ravages of his disease."

"But that doesn't prove him to be the Ripper."

"Quite so. It hardly seems possible that he could write the letters filled with American slang and crude errors in grammar and spelling which the Ripper sent to the authorities; letters containing information which could be known only by the murderer and the police. More to the point, Clarence was in Scotland at the time of one of the killings and at Sandringham when others took place. And there are equally firm reasons for exonerating suggested suspects close to him—his friend James Stephen and his physician, Sir William Gull."

"You've really studied up on this," Woods murmured. "I'd no idea you were so keen on it."

"And for good reason. I wasn't about to make a fool of myself by advancing an untenable notion. I don't believe the Ripper was a seaman, as some surmise, for there's not a scintilla of evidence to back the theory. Nor do I think the Ripper was a slaughterhouse worker, a midwife, a man disguised as a woman, or a London bobby. And I doubt the very existence of a mysterious physician named Dr. Stanley, out to avenge himself against the woman who had infected him, or his son."

"But there does seem to be a great number of medical men amongst the suspects," Woods said.

"Right you are, and for good reason. Consider the nature of the crimes—the swift and skillful removal of vital organs, accomplished in the darkness of the streets under constant danger of imminent discovery. All this implies the discipline of someone versed in anatomy, someone with the cool nerves of a practicing surgeon. Then, too, there's the matter of escaping detection. The Ripper obviously knew the alleys and byways of the East End so thoroughly that he could slip through police cordons and patrols without discovery. But if seen, who would have a better alibi than a respectable physician, carrying a medical bag on an emergency call late at night?"

"With that in mind, I set about my search, examining the rolls of London Hospital in Whitechapel Road. I went over the names of physicians and surgeons listed in the Medical Registry for that period."

"All of them?"

"It wasn't necessary. I knew what I was looking for—a surgeon who lived and practiced in the immediate Whitechapel area. Whenever possible, I followed up with a further investigation of my suspects' histories—researching hospital and clinic affiliations, even hobbies and background activities from medical journals, press reports and family records. Of course, all this takes a great deal of time and patience. I must have been tilting at this windmill for a good five years before I found my man."

Woods glanced at the nameplate on the bag. "J. Ridley, M.D.?"

"John Ridley. *Jack* to his friends—if he had any." Kane paused, thoughtful. "But that's just the point. Ridley appears to have had no friends and no family. An orphan, he received his degree from Edinburgh in 1878, ten years before the date of the murders. He set up private practice here in London, but there is no office address listed. Nor is there any further information to be found concerning him; it's as though he took particular care to suppress every detail of his personal and private life. This, of course, is what roused my suspicions. For an entire decade J. Ridley lived and practiced in the East End without a single mention of his name anywhere in print, except for his Registry listing. And after 1888, even *that* disappeared."

"Suppose he died?"

"There's no obituary on record."

Woods shrugged. "Perhaps he moved, emigrated, took sick, abandoned practice?"

"Then why the secrecy? Why conceal his whereabouts? Don't you see—it's the very lack of such ordinary details which leads me to suspect the extraordinary."

"But that's not evidence. There's no proof that your Dr. Ridley was the Ripper."

"That's why this is so important." Kane indicated the bag on the tabletop. "If we knew its history, where it came from———"

As he spoke, Kane reached down and picked up a brass letter opener from the table, then moved to the bag.

"Wait." Woods put a restraining hand on Kane's shoulder. "That may not be necessary."

"What do you mean?"

"I think the shopkeeper was lying. He knew what the bag contains—he had to, or else why did he fix such a ridiculous price? He never dreamed you'd take him up on it, of course. But there's no need for you to force the lock any more than there was for him to do so. My guess is that he has the key."

"You're right." Kane set the letter opener down. "I should have realized, if I'd taken the time to consider his reluctance. He must have the key." He lifted the shiny bag and turned. "Come along—let's get back to him before the shop closes. And this time we won't be put off by any excuses."

Dusk had descended as Kane and his companion hastened through the streets, and darkness was creeping across the deserted silence of Saxe-Coburg Square when they arrived.

They halted then, staring into the shadows, seeking the spot where the shop nestled between the residences looming on either side. The shadows were deeper here and they moved closer, only to stare again at the empty gap between the two buildings.

The shop was gone.

Woods blinked, then turned and gestured to Kane. "But we were here—we *saw* it————"

Kane didn't reply. He was staring at the dusty, rubble-strewn surface of the space between the structures; at the weeds which sprouted from the bare ground beneath. A chill night wind echoed through the emptiness. Kane stooped and sifted a pinch of dust between his fingers. The dust was cold, like the wind that whirled the fine grains from his hand and blew them away into the darkness.

"What happened?" Woods was murmuring. "Could we both have dreamed————?"

Kane stood erect, facing his friend. "This isn't a dream," he said, gripping the black bag.

"Then what's the answer?"

"I don't know." Kane frowned thoughtfully. "But there's only one place where we can possibly find it."

"Where?"

"The 1888 Medical Registry lists the address of John Ridley as Number 17 Dorcas Lane."

The cab which brought them to Dorcas Lane could not enter its narrow accessway. The dim alley beyond was silent and empty, but Kane plunged into it without hesitation, moving along the dark passage between solid rows of grimy brick. Treading over the cobblestones, it seemed to Woods that he was being led into another era, yet Kane's progress was swift and unfaltering.

"You've been here before?" Woods said.

"Of course." Kane halted before the unlit entrance to Number 17, then knocked.

The door opened—not fully, but just enough to permit the figure behind it to peer out at them. Both glance and greeting were guarded.

"Whatcher want?"

Kane stepped into the fan of light from the partial opening. "Good evening. Remember me?"

"Yes." The door opened wider and Woods could see the squat shadow of the middle-aged woman who nodded up at his companion. "Yer the one what rented the back vacancy last Bank 'oliday, ain'tcher?"

"Right. I was wondering if I might have it again."

"I dunno." The woman glanced at Woods.

"Only for a few hours." Kane reached for his wallet. "My friend and I have a business matter to discuss."

"Business, eh?" Woods felt the unflattering appraisal of the landlady's beady eyes. "Cost you a fiver."

"Here you are."

A hand extended to grasp the note. Then the door opened fully, revealing the dingy hall and the stairs beyond.

"Mind the steps now," the landlady said.

The stairs were steep and the woman was puffing as they reached the upper landing. She led them along the creaking corridor to the door at the rear, fumbling for the keys in her apron.

"'Ere we are."

The door opened on musty darkness, scarcely dispelled by the faint illumination of the overhead fixture as she switched it on. The landlady nodded at Kane. "I don't rent this for lodgings no more—it ain't properly made up."

"Quite all right." Kane smiled, his hand on the door.

"If there's anything you'll be needing, best tell me now. I've got to run over to the neighbor for a bit—she's been took ill."

"I'm sure we'll manage." Kane closed the door, then listened for a moment as the landlady's footsteps receded down the hall.

"Well," he said. "What do you think?"

Woods surveyed the shabby room with its single window framed by yellowing curtains. He noted the faded carpet with its pattern well-nigh worn away, the marred and chipped surfaces of the massive old bureau and heavy Morris chair, the brass bed covered with a much-mended spread, the ancient gas log in the fireplace framed by a cracked marble mantlepiece, and the equally cracked washstand fixture in the corner.

"I think you're out of your mind," Woods said. "Did I understand correctly that you've been here before?"

"Exactly. I came several months ago, as soon as I found the address in the Registry. I wanted a look around."

Woods wrinkled his nose. "More to smell than there is to see."

"Use your imagination, man! Doesn't it mean anything to you that you're standing in the very room once occupied by Jack the Ripper?"

Woods shook his head. "There must be a dozen rooms to let in this old barn. What makes you think this is the right one?"

"The Registry entry specified 'rear'. And there are no rear accommodations downstairs—that's where the kitchen is located. So this *has* to be the place."

Kane gestured. "Think of it—you may be looking at the very sink where the Ripper washed away the traces of his butchery, the bed in which he slept after his dark deeds were performed! Who knows what sights this room has seen and heard—the voice crying out in a tormented night-mare————"

"Come off it, Hilary!" Woods grimaced impatiently. "It's one thing to use your imagination, but quite another to let your imagination use you."

"Look." Kane pointed to the far corner of the room. "Do you see those indentations in the carpet? I noticed them when I examined this room on my previous visit. What do they suggest to you?"

Woods peered dutifully at the worn surface of the carpet, noting the four round evenly spaced marks. "Must have been another piece of furniture in that corner. Something heavy, I'd say."

"But what sort of furniture?"

"Well———" Woods considered. "Judging from the space, it wasn't a sofa or chair. Could have been a cabinet, perhaps a large desk———"

"Exactly. A rolltop desk. Every doctor had one in those days." Kane sighed. "I'd give a pretty penny to know what became of that item. It might have held the answer to all our questions."

"After all these years? Not bloody likely." Woods glanced away. "Didn't find anything else, did you?"

"I'm afraid not. As you say, it's been a long time since the Ripper stayed here."

"I didn't say that." Woods shook his head. "You may be right about the desk. And no doubt the Medical Registry gives a correct address. But all it means is that this room may once have been rented by a Dr. John Ridley. You've already inspected it once—why bother to come back?"

"Because now I have this." Kane placed the black bag on the bed. "And this." He produced a pocket knife.

"You intend to force the lock after all?"

"In the absence of a key I have no alternative." Kane wedged the blade under the metal guard and began to pry upwards. "It's important that the bag be opened here. Something it contains may very well be associated with this room. If we recognize the connection we might have an additional clue, a conclusive link———"

The lock snapped.

As the bag sprang open, the two men stared down at its contents—the jumble of vials and pillboxes, the clumsy old-style stethoscope, the probes and tweezers, the roll of gauze. And, resting atop it, the scalpel with the steel-tipped surface encrusted with brownish stains.

They were still staring as the door opened quietly behind them and the balding, elderly little man entered the room.

Kane frowned. "What do you want?"

"I'm afraid I must trouble you for my bag."

"But it's *my* property now—I bought it."

The little man sighed. "Yes, and I was a fool to permit it. I thought putting on that price would dissuade you. How was I to know you were a collector like myself?"

"Collector?"

"Of curiosa pertaining to murder." The little man smiled. "A pity you cannot see some of the memorabilia I've acquired. Not the commonplace items associated with your so-called Black Museum in Scotland Yard, but true rarities with historical significance." He gestured. "The silver jar in which the notorious French sorceress, La Voisin, kept her poisonous ointments; the actual daggers which dispatched the unfortunate nephews of Richard III in the Tower; yes, even the poker responsible for the atrocious demise of Edward II at Berkeley Castle on the night of September 21st, 1327. I had quite a bit of trouble locating it until I realized the date was reckoned according to the old Julian calendar."

Kane frowned impatiently "Who are you? What happened to that shop of yours?"

"My name would mean nothing to you. As for the shop, let us say that it exists spatially and temporally as I do—when and where necessary for my purposes. By your current and limited understanding, you might call it a sort of time machine."

Woods shook his head. "You're not making sense."

"Ah, but I am, and very good sense too. How else do you think I could pursue my interests so successfully unless I were free to travel in time? It is my particular pleasure to return to certain eras in this primitive past of yours, visiting the scenes of famous and infamous crimes and locating trophies for my collection."

"The shop, of course, is just something I used as a blind for this particular mission. It's gone now, and I shall be going too, just as soon as I retrieve my property. It happens to be the souvenir of a most unusual murder."

"You see?" Kane nodded at Woods. "I told you this bag belonged to the Ripper!"

"Not so," said the little man. "I already have the Ripper's murder weapon, which I retrieved directly after the slaying of his final victim on November 9th, 1888. And I can assure you that your Dr. Ridley was not Jack the Ripper but merely and simply an eccentric surgeon————" As he spoke, he edged toward the bed.

"No, you don't!" Kane turned to intercept him, but he was already reaching for the bag.

"Let go of that!" Kane shouted.

The little man tried to pull away, but Kane's hand swooped down frantically into the open bag and clawed. Then it rose, gripping the scalpel.

The little man yanked the bag away. Clutching it, he retreated as Kane bore down upon him furiously.

"Stop!" Woods cried. Hurling himself forward, he stepped between the two men, directly into the orbit of the descending blade.

There was a gurgle, then a thud, as he fell.

The scalpel clattered to the floor, slipping from Kane's nerveless fingers and coming to rest amidst the crimson stain that seeped and spread.

The little man stooped and picked up the scalpel. "Thank you," he said softly. "You have given me what I came for." He dropped the weapon into the bag.

Then he shimmered. Shimmered and disappeared.

But Wood's body didn't disappear. Kane stared down at it—at the throat ripped open from ear to ear.

He was still staring when they came and took him away.

The trial, of course, was a sensation. It wasn't so much the crazy story Kane told as the fact that nobody could even find the fatal weapon.

It was a most unusual murder. . . .

THE THIRD LEVEL

Jack Finney

The presidents of the New York Central and the New York, New Haven, and Hartford railroads will swear on a stack of timetables that there are only two. But I say there are three, because I've *been* on the third level at Grand Central Station.

Yes, I've taken the obvious step: I talked to a psychiatrist friend of mine, among others. I told him about the third level at Grand Central Station, and he said it was a waking-dream wish fulfillment. He said I was unhappy. That made my wife kind of mad, but he explained that he meant the modern world is full of insecurity, fear, war, worry, and all the rest of it, and that I just want to escape. Well, hell, who doesn't? Everybody I know wants to escape, but they don't wander down into any third level at Grand Central Station.

But that's the reason, he said, and my friends all agreed. Everything points to it, they claimed. My stamp collecting, for example—that's a "temporary refuge from reality." Well, maybe, but my grandfather didn't need any refuge from reality; things were pretty nice and peaceful in his day, from all I hear, and he started my collection. It's a nice collection, too, blocks of four of practically every United States issue, first-day covers, and so on. President Roosevelt collected stamps, too.

Anyway, here's what happened at Grand Central. One night last summer I worked late at the office. I was in a hurry to get uptown to my apartment, so I decided to use the subway from Grand Central because it's faster than the bus.

Now, I don't know why this should have happened to me. I'm just an ordinary guy named Charley, thirty-one years old, and I was wearing a tan gabardine suit and a straw hat with a fancy band—I passed a dozen men who looked just like me. And I wasn't trying to escape from anything; I just wanted to get home to Louisa, my wife.

I turned into Grand Central from Vanderbilt Avenue and went down the steps to the first level, where you take trains like the Twentieth Century. Then I walked down another flight to the second level, where the suburban trains leave from, ducked into an arched doorway headed for the subway— and got lost. That's easy to do. I've been in and out of Grand Central hundreds of times, but I'm always bumping into new doorways and stairs and corridors. Once I got into a tunnel about a mile long and came out in the lobby of the Roosevelt Hotel. Another time I came up in an office building on Forty-sixth Street, three blocks away.

Sometimes I think Grand Central is growing like a tree, pushing out new corridors and staircases like roots. There's probably a long tunnel that nobody knows about, feeling its way under the city right now, on its way to Times Square, and maybe another to Central Park. And maybe—because for so many people, through the years Grand Central *has* been an exit, a way of escape—maybe that's how the tunnel I got into . . . but I never told my psychiatrist friend about that idea.

The corridor I was in began angling left and slanting downward and I thought that was wrong, but I kept on walking. All I could hear was the empty sound of my own footsteps and I didn't pass a soul. Then I heard that sort of hollow roar ahead that means open space, and people talking. The tunnel turned sharp left; I went down a short flight of stairs and came out on the third level at Grand Central Station. For just a moment I thought I was back on the second level, but I saw the room was smaller, there were fewer ticket windows and train gates, and the information booth in the center was wood and old-looking. And the man in the booth wore a green eyeshade and long black sleeve protectors. The lights were dim and sort of flickering. Then I saw why: they were open-flame gaslights.

There were brass spittoons on the floor, and across the station a glint of light caught my eye: a man was pulling a gold watch from his vest pocket. He snapped open the cover, glanced at his watch, and frowned. He wore a dirty hat, a black four-button suit with tiny lapels, and he had a big, black, handlebar mustache. Then I looked around and saw that everyone in the station was dressed like 1890 something; I never saw so many beards, sideburns, and fancy mustaches in my life. A woman walked in through the train gate; she wore a dress with leg-of-mutton sleeves and skirts to the top of her high-buttoned shoes. Back of her, out on the tracks, I caught a glimpse of a locomotive, a very small Currier & Ives locomotive with a funnel-shaped stack. And then I knew.

To make sure, I walked over to a newsboy and glanced at the stack of papers at his feet. It was the *World;* and the *World* hasn't been published for years. The lead story said something about President Cleveland. I've found that front page since, in the Public Library files, and it was printed June 11, 1894.

I turned toward the ticket windows knowing that here—on the third level at Grand Central—I could buy tickets that would take Louisa and me anywhere in the United States we wanted to go. In the year 1894! And I wanted two tickets to Galesburg, Illinois.

Have you ever been there? It's a wonderful town still, with big old frame houses, huge lawns, and tremendous trees whose branches meet overhead and roof the streets. And in 1894, summer evenings were twice as long, and people sat out on their lawns, the men smoking cigars and talking quietly, the women waving palm-leaf fans, with the fireflies all around, in a peaceful world. To be back there with the First World War still twenty years off, and World War II over forty years in the future... I wanted two tickets for that.

The clerk checked the fare—he glanced at my fancy hatband, but he figured the fare—and I had enough for two coach tickets, one way. But when I counted out the money and looked up, the clerk was staring at me. He nodded at the bills. "That ain't money, mister," he said, "and if you're trying to skin me you won't get very far," and he glanced at the cash drawer beside him. Of course the money was old-style bills, half again as big as the money we use nowadays, and different-looking. I turned away and got out fast. There's nothing nice about jail, even in 1894.

And that was that. I left the same way I came, I suppose. Next day, during lunch hour, I drew $300 out of the bank, nearly all we had, and bought old-style currency (that *really* worried my psychiatrist friend). You can buy old money at almost any coin dealer's but you have to pay a premium. My $300 bought less than $200 in old-style bills, but I didn't care; eggs were thirteen cents a dozen in 1894.

But I've never again found the corridor that leads to the third level at Grand Central Station, although I've tried often enough.

Louisa was pretty worried when I told her all this and didn't want me to look for the third level anymore, and after awhile I stopped; I went back to my stamps. But now we're *both* looking, every weekend, because now we have proof that the third level is still there. My friend Sam Weiner disappeared! Nobody knew where, but I sort of suspected, because Sam's a city boy, and I used to tell him about Galesburg—I went to school there—and he always said he liked the sound of the place. And that's where he is, all right. In 1894.

Because one night, fussing with my stamp collection, I found—well, do you know what a first-day cover is? When a new stamp is issued, stamp collectors buy some and use them to mail envelopes to themselves on the very first day of sale; and the postmark proves the date. The envelope is called a first-day envelope. They're never opened; you just put blank paper in the envelope.

That night, among my oldest first-day covers, I found one that shouldn't have been there. But there it was. It was there because someone had mailed it to my grandfather at his home in Galesburg; that's what the address on the envelope said. And it had been there since July 18, 1894—the postmark showed that—yet I didn't remember it at all. The stamp was a six-cent, dull brown, with a picture of President Garfield. Naturally, when the envelope came to Granddad in the mail, it went right into his collection and stayed there— till I took it out and opened it.

The paper inside wasn't blank. It read:

> 941 Willard Street
> Galesburg, Illinois
> July 18, 1894
>
> Charley:
> I got to wishing that you were right. Then I got to *believing* you were right. And, Charley, it's true. I found the third level! I've been here two weeks, and right now, down the street at the Daly's, someone is playing a piano, and they're all out on the front porch singing *Seeing Nellie Home*. And I'm invited over for lemonade. Come on back, Charley and Louisa. Keep looking till you find the third level! It's worth it, believe me!

The note was signed Sam.

At the stamp and coin store I go to, I found out that Sam bought $800 worth of old-style currency. That ought to set him up in a nice little hay, feed, and grain business; he always said that's what he really wished he could do, and he certainly can't go back to his old business. Not in Galesburg, Illinois, in 1894. His old business? Why, Sam was my psychiatrist.